The Coral Wreck

Where the waters of the Philippine and Celebes Seas mingled under a leaden sky, a man fought for his life in the typhoon-swept waves. Thrown ashore at last, he lay unconscious. He was Dirk Rogers, schooner skipper, pearl diver and island rover.

When he opened his eyes, he stared up into a dark, fierce face – the face of Alimud Din whose crazy ambition to regain the fabulous Sword of Cordovada led Dirk into many wild adventures. How could he refuse to help this strange man in his quest? After all, Alimud Din had saved Dirk from certain death.

But there was more than a sword involved; there was gold: gold in a treasure ship thirty fathoms deep. Dirk Rogers was a deep-sea diver with no great lust for riches; Alimud Din was the opposite. How the duel between these two men was played out against a mysterious, tropical background makes unforgettable reading.

THE CORAL WRECK

Frank Crisp

Beaver Books

First published in 1964 by
Jonathan Cape Limited
30 Bedford Square, London WC1B 3EL

This paperback edition published in 1976 by
The Hamlyn Publishing Group Limited
London · New York · Sydney · Toronto
Astronaut House, Feltham, Middlesex, England
© Copyright Text Frank Crisp 1964
© Copyright Illustrations
The Hamlyn Publishing Group Limited 1976
ISBN 0 600 31914 8

Printed in England by Cox and Wyman Limited
London, Reading and Fakenham
Set in Intertype Plantin
Line drawings by Mike Jackson
Cover illustration by John Beswick

Contents

Chapter One

The Lone Swimmer

A typhoon was sweeping across Davao Gulf, breaching the coral-hemmed approaches to the Celebes Sea, and striking the peaks and ranges of Mindanao, second largest and southernmost island of the Philippines. The storm had travelled south through the island-dotted reaches of Micronesia, drenching and ravaging the land, exploding surf over reefs and low-lying atolls, driving great rollers over the deeps of the Philippine Sea. Then it had veered westwards to hit the steep-to shores of Mindanao.

Just a few hours before, the midday sun had been blazing down on a placid turquoise sea off Tinaca Point. South of here was a fifty-mile-wide submarine archipelago, reaching to the mainland of the Celebes, where the sea surface was broken by the scores of reefs and small islands which constituted the Sangihe Islands.

By this time, however – four o'clock on an August afternoon – the scene was dramatically changed. Here where the waters of the Philippine and Celebes seas mingled, the sky was dark with leaden cloud masses that drove like a panic-stricken mob before the fury of the wind. The typhoon was a monster looming over the cowering ocean, an invisible demon, a titanic sea genie that shrieked with a myriad voices. The islands trembled on their foundations, reefs that had glittered white in sunshine not long before were engulfed under the driving volume of grey-green seas that ran in fast, long, wind-flattened swells with spray licking at speed from their crests like bursts of steam.

Except for the shadow of an island to the south and the spectral loom of high land to the far north there was nothing but this great spread of tormented water oppressed and agitated by the demoniac wind. There was no ship or sail in sight, no birds even, for every bird was hugging itself in shelter on the coast. Over all that waste of angry water there was no vestige of life at all . . . save one solitary man, one lone and desperate swimmer.

He was drifting with wind and tide and, as the seas swept over him, his practically naked body glimmered with the bronze of long days in tropical suns. He was floating on his back mostly, swinging in the rushing seas, sometimes buried in a wave-top whipped over him by the tearing wind; but always he rose again to snatch a mouthful of air to stay afloat and to keep alive.

Time was passing for him in an increasing weariness, in a growing sea-sickness, with the thrash of wind and water deafening in his ears. Occasionally he would turn over and tread water for a while to ease his stiffening limbs. The sea was warm, but when he lifted his face to the wild wind it felt chill, cold as Arctic ice. He made no effort to swim. He was just keeping afloat; his sole purpose was to conserve his dwindling strength and somehow, by some fantastic chance, to last out the typhoon.

He was a young, strong man, but the endless hours in this muscle-wasting tumult would have sapped the energies of a giant. He counted the minutes in successive smothering wave-tops, the hours by the darkening sky, and every hour was a lifetime. Still he remained afloat, with the hungry fathoms beneath him waiting darkly for when he would lose consciousness, give up the struggle, and his aching lungs would fill with salt sea.

Darkness came early that night as the typhoon centre raged over the Sulu Archipelago to the west, over the palm-fringed beaches of Zamboanga, old-time city of pearls and slaves, and moved away into the South China Sea. Behind it the beaten seas began to rise, and off Tinaca Point the weary survivor began to toss in profound nerve-racking rollers, twenty feet high and more, black as pitch under a sky like ink.

It was like being battered in a revolving drum, and when the dark waters rolled over him he felt he must be going right down to the sea-bed; then he would suddenly surface again, and the cold night air would sting the salt on his face, a bitter rime that even the sea could not wash away.

Midnight came and passed, and it was two in the morning when a ghostly moon blinked through a cleft in the ravaged sky, spreading light like a milky mist over the brutal sea. The typhoon had gone as abruptly as it had arrived. Now a smooth breeze was blowing from the south over the still huge but dying seas.

The lone swimmer was still there, just kept afloat by an indomitable spirit to survive; but his mind was falling a prey to delirium. At times his limbs would feel fantastically bloated until he imagined he was some enormous tortured giant in the sea, with eyes stinging and inflamed, and an agony of thirst like a thistle growing in his throat.

Once he awakened to find himself swallowing water, a fathom deep with phosphorescent lights flashing about him, and he willed his nerveless limbs to drive him back to the surface where he gulped and gasped for air. And now he saw that the moon was grown full in a starlit sky and for a few moments his spirit rose on a wave of triumph. For he had beaten the typhoon! It was gone and he was still afloat!

The feeling did not last long. His exhausted body baffled his senses and his mind began to wander. In his delirium he heard the voices of friends and shipmates calling to him. He thought they were searching for him and he tried to shout, but no sound came from his parched throat. Then he saw a ship, his own ship, the *Jolo*, a little schooner, pale and white under the stars. But it passed on and vanished – a phantom of his imagination.

He could never recall the remaining dark hours of that night, for only instinct kept him afloat, and it was morning before his conscious mind awakened. By then the sun was above the horizon, already beating hard and strong on a sea fast gelatinising into a blue shimmering calm. He was on his back, automatically dragging in life-sustaining gulps of air. He blinked the salt from his eyes and gazed into an azure sky where there wasn't a single cloud.

An hour passed, and another, and only at times did a rare breeze ripple the flat sea. Then he thought he heard the sound of surf reaching him through the blue fathoms, a remote rustling roar. He thought it must be delirium again, but the sound persisted. At last he turned over to tread water and lift his head.

Some hundreds of yards distant over the slow-motion heave of the sea he saw a half-mile-long line of white surf, with here and there craggy outcrops of coral rock exposed. In the last few hours he had been in the grip of a tidal stream which was now carrying him along the edge of a reef.

For the first time in many hours he started swimming with a purpose, calling on his last vestiges of strength, dreading that the tide would sweep him past this forlorn refuge. But he need not have feared because the current was bearing him on to the reef – a living wall of coral anchored twenty fathoms deep on a volcanic uplift. Elsewhere, on either side of this struggling reef, there were great depths.

Soon he was lifting in curling breakers and his foot jagged against sharp coral. He was rolled over in the surf and his body was thrown against coral that cut like knives, and his blood stained the water. For a time he wallowed alongside the craggy, yellow, honeycombed reef edge, then his fingers gripped and he held on. Impervious to pain or of his own blood flowing from a score of cuts, he willed strength into his rubbery limbs and dragged his battered body over the edge of the reef flat.

He dried quickly in the breeze and soon the sun began to blister his salt-encrusted skin. A castaway thrown up by the sea he lay unconscious on the tidal flat among weeds and sea anemones, shellfish, snails and crustaceans. Sea-birds flighted over him and the surf sobbed and moaned at his feet. He was not much more than a youth, naked but for a pair of tattered trunks – a sailor, salvage man and pearl-diver – and his name was Dirk Rogers.

Chapter Two

In the Datu's House

Slowly the sun climbed to the zenith, but the castaway on the reef did not stir. During the afternoon clouds began to swell above the horizon to the east, cumbrous white cumuli sailing ponderously like the ghosts of vanished galleons, spreading ill-humoured shadows over the smooth waters.

The tide was rising and, calm though it was, the sea began to grow a little hostile along the reef edge. It thrashed and sobbed and began to lift fans of spray over the lonely survivor. He lay face down, head on his arms, his salt-whitened body blistering in the sun. Some distance away a school of porpoises began to snort and roll and, nearer at hand, in the channel close under the reef, two black-tipped fins showed. Below the fins were the blue-grey shapes of a pair of mako sharks.

Now spray was boosting regularly over the still form of Dirk Rogers. He stirred and groaned, and his mind groped darkly for a time before he opened his eyes. The fever of his thirst hit him like a knife-thrust. His hazy vision showed him the reef flat – a corrugated sea-sculptured expanse of coral about the width of a city highway, full of pools stirred mysteriously by the sudden movements of fish, eels and crabs. Beyond the reef was a stretch of surf-whitened water which extended into the blue of the deep sea.

A drenching shower of spray swept over Dirk and he forced himself on to his aching arms to look around. The sea within feet of him, rising hungrily to the ledge where he was lying. Within half an hour the reef would be awash, and in an hour it would be totally submerged.

He struggled to his knees and dragged himself a few yards farther on to the reef flat. He could do no more, for the effort exhausted him and he collapsed again into a dim, tormented world of semi-consciousness. Strange visions haunted his mind, nightmares interwoven with pleasant dreams. Giant creatures threatened to swallow him . . . cool waters invited him under shady palms. He heard voices . . . shrill hails from a great way off . . . then an urgent shout almost over him . . . and hands touched him!

He opened his eyes and stared up into a dark fierce face. His battered senses could not separate fantasy from reality. For here in front of him there had appeared a thickset dark-skinned man, dripping wet, wearing only a pair of shorts.

'Take heart, señor!' the man panted. 'The sea will not have you this time.'

Dirk could not speak a word in reply. He sat limply while the man looped a line under his arms. Then he lifted his wavering gaze and there, dangerously close to the reef, was a boat, a rough craft, a Moro vinta, a mere shell of a vessel with twin outriggers, tripod mast and a red triangular sail. There was a man in the stern sheets wielding a paddle to keep the boat's head into the wind, and a boy amidships was holding the line.

By now Dirk had realised that his rescuer was flesh and blood. Suddenly the man gave a yell of warning to his companions, then he dragged Dirk to the reef edge and together they were hauled towards the vinta. Dirk remembered coming alongside the lurching craft and its tangled odours of copra, fish, fruit and timber. Hands gripped him and he was dragged aboard practically insensible.

Later, when the vinta was under way again, he was aroused by someone offering him water from an earthenware bottle, and he recognised the man who had brought him off the reef. He tried to say something, but his swollen lips could form no words.

'There will be time to talk later, señor,' his rescuer said. 'We

are bound for the village of Jalna. We were on our way back from a
trading trip to Sarangani Bay when the typhoon forced us to run for
shelter. It is Fate that saved you, señor, for on our customary
route we would not have sighted you on the reef.'

Dirk nodded that he understood and drank a few mouthfuls of
the lukewarm water. His body was a mass of cuts from his contact
with the coral, but mostly he was suffering from the effects of
exposure, thirst and exhaustion. The other man and boy of the
boat's crew were sitting by the tiller apparently chattering about
him. These people were Moros – native seamen of the Sulu Archipelago and the Mindanao coasts. Moro was the old Spanish word
for Moor, a title the sixteenth-century Spaniards had given to the
tough Mohammedan seafarers of the Southern Philippines whom
they never succeeded in subduing. Vaguely, before he relapsed into
unconsciousness, Dirk saw that his rescuer was quite young, stocky
and muscular with black vigilant eyes and something of the wild
rapacity of his pirate forebears stamped on his features.

It was eventide, the fleeing twilight of the tropics, when the
vinta glided into a mangrove-linked creek in mountain-hemmed
Davao Gulf. Here was situated the poor fishing village of Jalna,
home of a remnant of the Minganoro tribe which, through econ-
omic and political pressures, had been driven to eke out a livelihood
on the sea-shore. Too insignificant to have an official mayor or
presidente, Jalna had as a headman the Moro datu who still retained this courtesy title as a descendant of a once proud and virile
ruling family which had fallen on evil days.

The village consisted of a score of bamboo huts and shacks, some
cargo sheds, a Chinese store, the timber house of the datu with its
carvings and sheltered verandah, and a small weather-beaten
mosque half-hidden amid the palms on the hill-side. On the other
bank of the wide creek there was a sawmill and a rickety jetty where
a motor barge was lying.

Shouts greeted the arrival of the vinta as it glided into the shallows like a bird folding its wings, and soon there was a lot of excitement and chatter among the village folk when they learned about
the rescue. Dirk was just semi-conscious when he was carried

ashore and taken to the house with the carved eaves and door-posts, the home of Suliman, the datu.

When he opened his eyes it was another day and past twelve o'clock, for his sleep of exhaustion had lasted eighteen hours. He was in a low, raftered room where sunshine streamed through an open window. It was warm but it seemed to be windy out of doors. He could hear a high breeze booming in the palms about the house. This was a curious room, half living quarters, half a sort of museum, for one entire wall was decorated with old and probably very valuable Moro weapons. Pride of place was held by two muzzle-loading muskets with elaborate silver-inlaid stocks. There was also a bronze shield and spears, a kris in an ivory sheath and various knives and curios, pathetic mementos of a glorious fighting past.

Dirk could see past a partly-drawn bamboo curtain on to the outside verandah. An elderly Moro, dressed in white tunic and trousers, and wearing a red fez, was sitting cross-legged at a low work-bench. He was busy engraving a brass bowl with simple well-worn tools.

Dirk was lying on a couch, still wearing only the same tattered swim-trunks, but there was a bandage on his right leg, another on his right forearm, and the cuts and bruises on his body had been treated with a salve. His mind was clear, but when he tried to sit up he was quickly aware of his aching body. He felt as though he had been sand-bagged all over. The sharp pains took him by surprise and he couldn't keep back a groan.

The old man at work on the verandah must have heard him, for he got to his feet and came into the room. He was of middle height, very dark skinned, with a stern heavily-lined face. He gazed at the bronzed young man on the couch for some moments without speaking, then a kindly smile transformed his austere features.

'Where am I?' Dirk inquired painfully.

'You are safe in the village of Jalna in Davao Gulf,' the old Moro said, speaking slowly in good English. 'I am Suliman, the village datu. This is my house and you are welcome here, my son.'

'I must thank you – for saving my life.'

'It is not I you have to thank but my son, Alimud Din. It was he who saw you and brought you off the reef.'

'You – must be wondering – how I ever got there,' Dirk said weakly.

'Allah brought you there, my son, but there is no need for you to talk so soon.' He clapped his hands smartly and an elderly woman, in a coloured gown, appeared discreetly from a rear doorway. The datu spoke to her in a Moro dialect, then he turned again to Dirk.

'You must eat and drink and gather strength, perhaps sleep again, then if you wish we can talk.'

'There's something I must ask you,' Dirk said urgently. 'Have you news of a motor schooner – the *Jolo*? She was – caught in the typhoon – off Tinaca Point!'

'Many small vessels foundered in the storm, I am told,' the datu replied. 'I will make inquiries for you. There is a coastguard station on Harun Head, higher up the coast. I will ask if there is news of this vessel you speak of.'

'Thank you. You are very kind,' Dirk said huskily.

The datu returned to his work and soon the woman appeared with a tray of food – coconut milk to drink, boiled crayfish, sweet potatoes and fresh bamboo shoots, some pineapple and mangoes.

Dirk didn't expect to sleep again that day, but he was mistaken for it was after dark when he awakened a second time. A pressure oil-lamp, suspended from one of the room's rafters, had been lighted, and outside on the verandah Dirk could see men's hunched shadowy figures in the glimmer of a hurricane-lamp, and he could hear their quiet voices.

He felt a great deal better on this second awakening. The meal had given him strength, and though his body still ached he was able to move without too much effort. He got up from the couch and called out softly.

'Datu!'

In a moment Suliman appeared in the doorway. When he saw Dirk on his feet he entered the room and turned up the pressure lamp.

'I can see you are recovered, my son. See, we have found clothes for you, and sandals which I think will fit.' He indicated a pair of white shorts and a cotton shirt and some sandals by the side of the couch. 'Put them on and join us outside.'

Left alone again, Dirk slipped on the clothes, then he went out on to the verandah where he found two other men sitting cross-legged with the datu about a low coffee table called a tabak. A small coffee urn was kept hot on a tiny charcoal brazier. The lights of a few lamps could be seen in the village, and one was moving along the foreshore where a fisherman was checking his boat. The moon was showing over the shoulder of Harun Head, a jungle-covered promontory higher up the coast, and it was spreading silver light across the waters of Davao Gulf, but the creek and the village were still immersed in a soft darkness.

'Come and sit with us, my son,' the datu said, hospitably indicating a place on his rug.

'Did you have news of the *Jolo*?' Dirk asked.

'I have good news. A schooner of that name put into Tawan harbour yesterday morning, and she is there now repairing storm damage. Tawan is just a few miles on the other side of Harun Head.'

'Were any of her crew lost?'

'Tawan harbour-master says the *Jolo* reported the loss of her skipper.'

'I am the *Jolo*'s skipper,' Dirk informed his host. 'My name is Dirk Rogers.'

'This much I guessed for myself,' the datu replied, 'and I have already sent word from the coastguard station that we will bring you to Tawan tomorrow.' Before Dirk could say any more the datu began to introduce his companions. He turned first to a thin active-looking little man with somewhat furtive eyes, a yellow-hued face and black sleek moustaches. 'This is my friend, Miguel Gomez, overseer of the timber station across the creek.'

Gomez had on a striped shirt, white trousers and a crumpled wide-brimmed hat. He was a Filipino, but Dirk guessed he had Chinese and Spanish blood in his veins as well. The man acknowledged Dirk's greeting with a sly but pleasant smile. 'I am pleased to make your acquaintance, Señor Rogers. Congratulations on your escape from the sea.'

'And here is my son, Alimud Din,' the datu added.

This time Dirk looked into the shadowed face of the young Moro who had rescued him. Alimud Din was sturdy and muscular, sombre of face, with an alert gaze which could flash suddenly with a fanatical glitter.

'My thanks for saving my life,' Dirk said sincerely.

Alimud Din shrugged his shoulders. 'It was only what any man would have done, señor.'

Dirk was handed a cup of strong black coffee. 'Let me tell you about myself and what happened to me,' he said, for he could see his companions were eager to know, but after their fashion they would not ask him questions. 'I am master of the motor schooner, *Jolo*. My partner, Jim Cartwright, and I are in the pearling and salvage business, and on the day of the typhoon we were working off Tinaca Point prospecting for new pearling grounds.'

'So it is true you are a diving man!' Alimud Din interrupted.

'Has not Señor Rogers just said so?' the datu said sharply to his son.

Alimud Din paid no attention to this rebuke. 'This is surely Allah's doing – that I should rescue a diving man – in fulfilment of my dream!' he said in a fierce whisper. In the light of the wavering hurricane-lamp his features were set like bronze and his eyes glimmered with the flame of some secret desire close to his heart. 'This is surely Allah's doing,' he said again in the same tense whisper.

'Have you no manners at all? Let our guest tell his story in his own way,' the datu commanded. 'Please continue,' he said, turning his calm smile on Dirk.

But Gomez had a question too. 'Did you find new pearling grounds, señor?' he inquired with his sly grin.

Dirk chuckled and shook his head. 'No, but we did find something almost as good – a deep channel where the tides have drifted old oyster-shell until it has grown into a bed a fathom thick. It lies deep – two hundred feet or more.'

'You have dived to this great depth – *two hundred feet!*' Alimud Din exclaimed eagerly.

Dirk nodded. 'If that channel is worked with the right gear pearl-shell can be raised by the ton to show a handsome profit.'

'Pearl-shell is no use to the small man,' Gomez said, shaking his head sadly. 'The poor man needs to find pearls, then in one day he can be rich.'

'Some are chosen to be rich. It is Fate,' the datu said evenly.

'Fate, Allah or the Prophet – which of them speaks to a man in his dreams?' Alimud Din remarked uneasily. 'A man can deny such a voice only at his peril!'

Dirk glanced curiously at the young Moro. He did not understand the man's meaning, but he was sure that the datu and Miguel Gomez did.

'A man cannot live for long on dreams, my son. That way lies madness,' the datu said firmly. 'Be silent and let the young captain tell us how he was lost in the typhoon.'

'There's not a lot to tell,' Dirk said. 'We were working a dozen miles south of Tinaca Point when the typhoon struck. We had picked up a radio warning the previous night, but we reckoned the big wind would go far to the east of us. It must have veered sharp west during the night.

'I was diving – riding the anchor – using just a wide-view helmet strapped to my shoulders with a lifeline and an airhose to the ship.'

'You mean the anchor had been lowered close to the sea-bed and you were riding on it?' Gomez queried with a lift of his black eyebrows.

'It's a quick way of prospecting for pearl-shell, and it allows a diver to use a telephone,' Dirk explained. 'The ship drifts with the tide, and if the diver sights pearl-shell he phones the deck and the anchor is lowered to the bottom.

'I was down about ten fathoms and we had just moved over some difficult ground where there were a lot of coral heads and snags spearing up from the bottom. I was getting anxious when what I feared actually happened – my airhose fouled a coral head! The schooner was drifting at a walking pace. I phoned the deck and my partner, Jim, threw over a lot of slack to prevent the airhose parting. Then they lowered the anchor. By then I'd fouled my lifeline too.

'Of course I could have jettisoned my gear and reached the surface,' Dirk continued, 'but ten fathoms is a long way up on one breath and besides I wanted to save my equipment if I could. I was still trying to clear my lines when the sea darkened as the typhoon hit the schooner. After that things happened faster than we could cope with them. The schooner's anchor cable parted and Jim phoned to say they couldn't hold her over me with the motor. Then I knew it was time to cut myself loose. I unlatched my weights, threw off the helmet and started up on a lungful of air.

'When I broke surface I was in the middle of the typhoon. I never even saw the schooner again. The seas were driving before a terrific wind. All I could do was stay afloat. I drifted and floated and swam for the rest of that day, all through the night, and next morning I was carried on to the reef where Alimud Din found me.'

'In that time you must have covered thirty sea miles,' Gomez said. 'It was a noble effort to stay afloat in such weather.'

'I owe my life to Alimud Din. Some day I may be able to repay him,' Dirk said, looking at the Moro sailor.

'Who knows when that day may come,' Alimud Din commented briefly.

After Dirk had told his story the datu's wife called them to an evening meal, a very good meal in honour of the guest. There was roast chicken, baked camotes, various greens and more coffee. When the meal was over the datu informed Dirk that he would be taken to Tawan to rejoin his ship early next morning in Alimud Din's vinta, as there was no proper road along the coast from Jalna.

Then Gomez prepared to leave for his bungalow at the timber station on the other side of the creek, and Dirk, feeling some fresh air would complete his recovery, offered to accompany the overseer as far as the head of the creek. It was now bright moonlight and the softest of breezes was swaying the tops of the palms.

Gomez looked surprised but pleased at Dirk's suggestion. Though the little Filipino seemed at first to have a sly and suspicious look, yet some hidden integrity in the man's character appealed to the younger pearl-diver.

As they followed the path through coconut groves close by the creek they talked again of Dirk's escape and of his rescue by Alimud Din.

'He is a brave man,' Dirk remarked.

'Brave like most of his race,' Gomez answered, 'but sick with bitterness too. The datu and his family are descended from ancient rulers of this land. The datu's great-grandfather was the Sultan Alimud Din of the Minganoro Moros. If you go into the hills, at the head of Lajaka Valley, you will find the ruins of the tribe's fortress. Once the family ruled the entire province, commanded a thousand warriors and a fleet of vintas.'

'It's a sad thing for them to be reduced to living as fishermen,' Dirk said.

'Sad but inevitable, señor. Their ways were good for them but not for their slaves and enemies. The datu is resigned, but his son will never be resigned. He lives on dreams and hopes of being rich and powerful again. There can be no cure for such a one but fortune, no peace but death. He talks of fables as though they were truth. In everything that happens he reads a sign that Allah will restore his family's fortunes.'

'I owe him my life. I'll help him if I can,' Dirk said.

They had reached a primitive bridge across the upper reaches of the creek and here Dirk decided to turn back. Fireflies were looping golden tassels in a bank of shrubs and nipa palms by the water's edge. Tree crickets and frogs made weird orchestrations in the mangrove swamps.

Gomez held out his hand with a flourish. 'I am the datu's friend, señor. I would like to be your friend too, so I ask you to be careful.'

'Careful – of what?'

'Of Alimud Din's fables. Already I know he sees you as part of a fable.'

'Surely you're not going to leave me with a riddle like that,' Dirk said with a laugh.

Gomez smiled humourlessly in the moonlight. 'I cannot say more because I am the datu's friend, but if Alimud Din speaks, then you will know what I mean, and you will remember that I asked you to walk carefully. Help him if you wish, but be wary, for I'm sure he is a little mad.'

Chapter Three

A Moro Legend

When Dirk got back to the datu's house Alimud Din was waiting for him on the verandah. The hurricane-lamp was turned out. It was no longer necessary because moonlight made a mirror of the creek waters and lit up the entire village. Alimud Din was standing like a statue beside one of the carved verandah pillars which had been hewn from a bread-fruit tree.

'What time do we start in the morning?' Dirk inquired.

'At first light, señor. It is not far to Tawan, but I have no engine in my boat, and if the wind is not favourable it is difficult to weather Harun Head.'

'In that case I think I'll get some sleep,' Dirk said.

'I have been waiting for you, señor. My father has already gone to his bed.' Alimud Din rested a sinewy hand on Dirk's forearm. He stared into the young diver's face with a sort of sinister excitement. 'Did I hear you right when you said you had dived *two hundred feet deep* to look for pearls?'

'That is true.'

'It is a great depth for a man to go,' Alimud Din murmured wonderingly, as though wishing to be reassured in some burning hope.

'I've been a long way deeper at times,' Dirk told him.

'Did you not lose your equipment in the typhoon? Did you not cut loose from it to escape to the surface?' the Moro asked concernedly.

24

'My partner and I have plenty of equipment. Diving is our business.'

'Ah, so you have more in the schooner at Tawan where your partner awaits you,' Alimud Din said with real relief.

'Of course, but tell me what's troubling you,' Dirk said straightforwardly. 'You've only got to say and I'll help you.'

'Señor, there is a task before me that is beyond my own powers. It is a thing before me as a duty, though some will not believe it. And though it is beyond my own powers, señor, it is a thing you can do with your special equipment.'

'So you want me to dive somewhere,' Dirk said.

'Ah, I want to ask a great favour, but you see my position. I have no money. I cannot pay you like these worthless upstart traders who buy your pearl-shell.'

'They're honest traders.'

'So you say, for you have a kind heart. You do not understand. This is my country, my people's country!' Alimud Din waved a hand at the jungle behind them. 'I am descended from sultans and here I am a beggarly fisherman without a gold piece to pay for a favour. What am I to offer you – a handful of fish? Will you go out of your way for that?'

'There's no question of money between us,' Dirk said. 'Tell me what you wish me to do.'

'Ah, you are a noble man, Dirk Rogers. By the Prophet, it warms my heart to find one among so many that thinks nothing of money.'

'What do you want me to do?' Dirk asked.

The Moro's eyes narrowed like shutters closing over a flame, and his dark smile seemed moulded about his lips. 'Come into the house, señor, I have something to show you.'

He led the way into the low-beamed apartment at the front of the datu's house where the couch Dirk would sleep on was set by the window. Alimud Din turned up the light of the pressure lamp.

'My father is asleep. He is old and tired and his mind grows dim. I do not wish to worry him with ambitions he can never share, so let us be very quiet.'

Dirk waited, full of wonder, as the Moro went to a bronze casket standing on an ebony table. He took a key from the casket, then turned his attention to a large mahogany chest against the inner wall. He inserted the key in the lock, turned it gently and opened the lid.

Dirk saw that the chest was crammed with scrolls of parchment. After some deliberation Alimud Din selected one of these and brought it to a tabak in the middle of the floor where he seated himself on a rug. He motioned for Dirk to join him.

'That chest is old, señor, centuries old, and some of the scrolls it contains are older. They are records of our family and tribe from time immemorial, since the first Mohammedan teacher landed on these shores and converted my forefathers to Islam.' Alimud Din spoke in a confidential whisper as his strong nervous fingers reverently unrolled the yellowed parchment under the inadequate glow of the lamp.

Somehow Dirk could not help feeling like an unwilling conspirator here in the quiet shadowy room, talking with this strange zealous Moro of whom he knew so little except that he'd saved his life. The stillness was broken only by the sinister rustle of lizards in the roof, the sough of the night wind in the moonlit palms outside and, more remotely, by the distant wash of the sea on the sandy foreshore.

Alimud Din unrolled the scroll and displayed faded reams of Arabic writings which were totally unintelligible to Dirk.

'My father is learned in the Arabic script,' the Moro whispered, 'and I myself can read it tolerably well. But this writing I know by heart, for my father has read these scripts to me since I was a boy.'

Alimud Din rested his forefinger on a certain paragraph and raised his eyes to meet Dirk's curious gaze. Without looking at the script he went on:

'Here it is written, señor ... *In the year 1734 in the Christian calendar, when Harun al Rashid was Sultan of Minganoro, a Spanish castaway of noble blood was thrown upon the shores of his domain. The Spaniard's name was Don Carlos Legaspi, and it is said he carried with him the fabulous Sword of Cordovada of which*

26

a legend is told that he who holds the sword will know its secret and become the possessor of boundless wealth.'

Dirk made no comment. He waited as Alimud Din carefully rolled up the scroll, fastened the leather thong about it, then raised his eyes again.

'Señor, it is my lifelong ambition to find the Sword of Cordovada,' he stated simply.

Dirk did not dare smile at the other's strange faith. 'How can you be sure it really exists?' he inquired.

At this remark the Moro seemed to contain his feelings with difficulty. 'Señor, there is a story about Don Carlos Legaspi which has been handed down by word of mouth in our family for more than two centuries. The story tells where the Sword of Cordovada may be found, and here in this manuscript is proof of its existence in black and white, as you have seen with your own eyes!'

'If that is so why hasn't the sword been claimed?' Dirk asked, careful to humour the other.

Alimud Din smiled knowingly. 'That's very easily answered. No one has ever been able to reach the sword – until Allah sent you. You, Señor Rogers, you can find the Sword of Cordovada. And I ask only this of you – just one single day of your time!'

Dirk hardly knew what to say. He didn't want to offend the man, for he felt indebted to him, but it was the wildest request that had ever been made of him.

'I can't guarantee to find this sword,' he said sincerely. 'No doubt a man called Don Carlos Legaspi did exist, but this tale about the Sword of Cordovada which he was supposed to possess – it's a legend!'

'I ask for no guarantees!' Alimud Din said almost pleadingly. 'I only ask for one day of your time. Is that too much for saving your life?'

'I willingly give you many days of my time, Alimud Din. Where does the sword lie?'

The Moro smiled with relief, but he was suddenly cautious. 'Let us sleep on our friendship, señor, and tomorrow when we reach Tawan I will speak again. We must go first to Tawan, for is not your diver's equipment there? And who knows, your partner may talk you out of your goodness and I would have shared my secret to no avail?'

Alimud Din returned the scroll to its place, locked the chest and put the key away in the casket. 'I ask one more favour, Señor Rogers – that you say nothing of this to my father. He would not understand. He would think we were foolhardy, for he has not my own faith in our destiny.'

'I will say nothing to your father,' Dirk promised.

As soon as Alimud Din had gone he took off his clothes, turned down the lamp and lay down on the couch. It was a long time before he got to sleep, because he had the uncanny feeling he'd somehow slipped back into another age and was going to have some difficulty getting out of it.

Dirk was up at first light next morning. He washed in a water tub behind the house and dressed himself in the ill-fitting shirt and trousers the datu had kindly lent him. Then he was called to a meal of broiled fish, rice bread and coffee on the verandah.

After the meal Dirk thanked the datu for his hospitality and said goodbye. He walked down through the rustling palm grove to the shore, watched by the villagers and accompanied by a few curious children. Then he waded out over the sandy shallows to where the vinta was lying at anchor with Alimud Din aboard, quite alone.

After a greeting and a few remarks about the weather, which appeared to be favourable enough, Alimud Din hauled up the anchor; then he and Dirk each took a paddle and they moved the light craft out into the mouth of the creek. As they began to feel the heave of the blue rollers they hoisted the big red sail; and this was why the vessel had twin outriggers, for it had no keel and would have capsized under the pressure of so much canvas.

The wind was from the north, so they put the craft on a port tack and Alimud Din steered well out to sea. When at length they drew abeam of Harun Head they dipped the sail, then bore landwards on a starboard tack. Far out in the Gulf a white-hulled cargo liner was heading for Davao. Closer at hand two small inter-island ships were in view and a few vinta and prau sails dotted the blue seascape.

Tawan came in sight as soon as they rounded Harun Head. It was a nondescript sleepy little harbour just large enough to accommodate the smaller coastal vessels. There was a harbour road with the customary collection of cargo sheds and warehouses, and behind that a straggling street, lined with open-fronted shops, leading into an open market-place. A solitary road ran away along the flat coastal strip to the north, picked out with drunken telegraph-poles spaced at long intervals. The harbour was contained by a breakwater and a concrete pier.

From a long way off Dirk got his eyes on his own schooner, the *Jolo*, where she lay tied up astern of a big sea-going Buginese prau. There were men at work on her, but they were unaware of the vinta approaching because Alimud Din had brought the vessel close inshore.

They tied up the vinta by some harbour steps and made their way along the pier. Dirk gave a hail as he approached the *Jolo*. Jim Cartwright, his partner, was supervising the schooner's three Malay deck-hands in re-rigging the foremast. At Dirk's hail he dropped his gear and jumped on to the pier to greet his skipper.

Jim was a fair-haired, lean, tough, hard-working fellow whom the sea had made old in experience. He was wearing a singlet, blue dungarees and a white peaked cap.

'It's good to set eyes on you again, Dirk!' he exclaimed feelingly, as he seized his skipper's hand. 'When we lost you out there off Tinaca Point, I thought it was your day to die.'

'I reckon I wasn't born to be drowned, Jim. The sea throws me ashore every time. It set my heart at rest when I heard you'd made it into Tawan with the ship.'

Jim nodded. 'A message came through from the coastguard station on Harun Head to say you were safe. Come aboard and have some coffee while you tell me what happened.'

'Why, first of all, Jim, I want you to meet a friend of mine,' Dirk said. 'He saved my life. If it hadn't been for him I'd have been shark bait for sure.' He turned to Alimud Din, who was standing, smiling smoothly, a few paces in the rear, and he introduced the Moro to his partner.

Alimud Din looked at Dirk. 'Señor, I will not come aboard just yet. There is a man in the town I wish to see. You will not forget your promise! We can leave Tawan at midday and still be back before sunset. It is not too much to ask.'

'I won't forget. It will be all right,' Dirk said reassuringly.

'What's he talking about?' Jim asked curiously as Alimud Din went off towards the harbour road.

'It's an involved tale, Jim,' the pearler skipper said with a wry smile, 'and I'm not so sure I've got it right myself yet, but I'll tell you what I know over a cup of coffee in the cabin.'

They boarded the *Jolo* and Dirk greeted the crew. They were men who had been signed on in Davao for a single pearling trip. Then he looked around his typhoon-battered vessel. She was a sturdy two-masted schooner of rock elm and East India teak, fitted with an auxiliary diesel engine.

'At any rate we have a sound boat and half a cargo of pearl-shell that ought to pay our expenses for the trip,' the skipper said.

They went below into the schooner's saloon cabin, and, while Dirk got into some of his own clothes, Jim made coffee. Then, seated at the cabin table, with his back against a bulkhead, Dirk told his partner all that had happened to him since that desperate moment, ten fathoms deep, when he'd cut his lines, jettisoned his gear, and made for the storm-swept surface on a lungful of air. He went on to describe what he remembered of his rescue by Alimud Din, his arrival at Jalna, and his night at the datu's house. He ended his story with an account of Alimud Din's request and his own promise to the Moro to whom he owed his life.

'The Sword of Cordovada,' Jim remarked with a disapproving frown when he'd heard this last episode. 'It sounds sheer fantasy. It's the wildest notion I've ever heard. I suppose this crazy Moro thinks if he gets the sword it will make him the richest man in the Philippines.'

'I'd say that was his idea, Jim.'

'And where are you supposed to look for the sword?'

'That he hasn't told me as yet. It can't be far away. You heard him say if we left at midday we could be back by sunset.'

'Why doesn't he just go and get the thing himself?' Jim demanded.

'Because only a diver can get it!'

'So Cordovada's Sword is supposed to be somewhere under water!' Jim said with an incredulous smile. 'Are you really going to waste your time like this? You know as well as I do the yarn's just moonshine!'

'Maybe I do, Jim, but don't forget that Alimud Din saved my life. I can't do less than give up a day of my time for him. Besides, legends and folk-tales go along with the country, so to speak, like the flora and fauna. Sometimes you've just got to accept them, for a time anyhow.'

'I don't know what that means to you, Dirk, but it doesn't make much sense to me,' Jim said in his practical fashion.

'I just don't want to ride rough-shod over Alimud Din's dreams and hopes,' Dirk explained.

Soon they went on deck again and Dirk made a thorough inspection of the ship, but apart from minor storm damage, which Jim and the crew were busy repairing, the schooner was in good shape and there was nothing to worry about her seaworthiness. Presently Alimud Din returned and he was asked to join Dirk and Jim in the saloon cabin for a meal which their Malay cook had prepared.

'Well, what's it to be? D'you still want me to go after the Sword of Cordovada?' Dirk said to the Moro when they had seated themselves in the cabin.

'Señor, I am depending on you. I have waited all my life for this day. Have you confided in your partner?'

'I've told Jim as much as I know myself,' Dirk answered.

'Good, then it only remains for me to recount the tradition of the Minganoro Moros – for it is in the tradition that the place is named,' Alimud Din stated. He clasped his hands together and a tense brooding expression, which by this time Dirk knew well, fastened inexorably on his dark face.

Though breezy outside it was hot and humid in the *Jolo*'s cabin and the temperature stood in the high eighties. Clouds were drifting over the Gulf and every now and then sunlight, slanting through the cabin skylights, would be darkened as though by evil portent; and at such moments the boom of surf on the outer reefs would swell louder in the background.

Chapter Four

The Sacred Well

Alimud Din broke straight into his story.

'As it is written in the archives of my tribe, which you saw with your own eyes last night, Señor Rogers, over two centuries ago, in the year 1734, a Spaniard called Don Carlos Legaspi was thrown as a castaway upon the shores of South Mindanao, not very far from here.'

Alimud Din looked from one to the other of his listeners to assure himself of their earnest attention, but indeed the fevered way the man talked, and the avid gleam in his eyes, couldn't fail to secure their interest in his tale.

'This Spaniard was taken prisoner by the Minganoro tribe. At first they would have killed him because for over two hundred years there had been bitter war between the Spaniards and the Moros; but Don Carlos, though starved, exhausted and broken by a long sea voyage, convinced them he was a man of noble birth, related to the Spanish governor of Manila. So he was taken before the Sultan Harun al Rashid in the fortress at the head of Lajaka Valley.'

Alimud Din stuck out a muscular arm and pointed towards the shore.

'The ruins of that fortress still stand, not ten miles from here, betwixt Tawan and Jalna,' he said dramatically. Then in a softer tone he continued. 'It was decided to hold Don Carlos to ransom. He was kept prisoner in the fortress and well treated, but before he recovered from his fatigue he fell sick with a fever. In his delirium he confided in his jailer whom he mistook for one of his lost companions. He talked of Cordovada's Sword – a sword with a hilt inlaid with gold and housed in an ivory scabbard – which he said he had brought with him on his voyage from the East. Many times during his fever Don Carlos stated that this sword held the secret of boundless wealth.

'Of course, the jailer asked where the wonderful sword could be found, but even in his delirium Don Carlos was faithful to some great promise he had made. He said the sword must be carried to his kinsman, the governor of Manila, and that he had hidden it somewhere on the beach, for he had known he had been cast ashore in the country of Spain's deadly enemies, the Mohammedan Moros.

'The jailer told his master, Sultan al Rashid, all that he had gleaned from Don Carlos's delirium. Then others were sent to the Spaniard, while he was still sick, pretending to be his friends and countrymen, but he would not tell where the sword was hidden.

'At last, when Don Carlos recovered, the sultan demanded that he reveal where this famous Sword of Cordovada was hid, but Don Carlos denied all knowledge of it. He said it was an illusion of his sickness and that no such sword existed. Threats of death and torture were of no avail, so Harun al Rashid planned to obtain by cunning what he could not have by force.

'There was another Spaniard in the hands of the Moros, and this man, under pain of death, played the traitor. He was allowed to pass word to Don Carlos how he might escape and reach a village on the shore where friendly natives would carry him to the Spanish fortress at Zamboanga.

'Many weeks had passed,' Alimud Din explained, continuing his tale, 'and Don Carlos was weary of captivity, and no word had ever come that his ransom would be paid. So he decided to try this way of escape and of course Harun al Rashid saw to it that he succeeded.

'One night Don Carlos and the traitor Spaniard were allowed to steal out of the fortress and beyond the outer walls. They made their way to the sea-shore and, as Harun al Rashid had suspected,

Don Carlos made a detour to seek the sword he had concealed close by the beach. As soon as he had retrieved the sword the traitor seized hold of him and some of the sultan's guards came running along the beach.

'Don Carlos, made desperate by his betrayal, killed the traitor and began to climb a hill trail leading into the mountains. He was pursued by the guards and at last he found himself trapped and surrounded in Kala Valley, a place which for ages past had been famed for its deep springs of pure water. One of these had been a sacred place for the ancient peoples who dwelt in the land before the Moros. It was even then known as the Sacred Well. There Don Carlos was surrounded by the sultan's soldiers. He knew he must die and his only thought was to put the Sword of Cordovada beyond the reach of his enemies.

'Don Carlos held the sword aloft in its ivory scabbard. He laughed at the guards and he called to them that he who would know the secret must follow him. Then he plunged into the Sacred Well and was never seen again.'

Alimud Din had told his tale quickly and smoothly. Now he sat still and marble-faced for a little while, with just the glitter of his eyes to indicate his pent-up feelings.

'Now I understand,' Dirk said. 'You want me to dive into the Sacred Well of Kala Valley.'

'Señor, the well is deep – far too deep for any man to plumb unaided.'

'How deep is it?'

'One hundred and seventy feet, Señor Rogers. I am certain of the depth for often I have lowered a weighted rope to the bottom. No man, not the greatest pearl-diver that ever lived, could dive so far unaided, but you, Señor Rogers, with your equipment, you can reach the bottom quickly. You only have to descend, retrieve the sword from the bottom and return at once to the surface.'

'You seem very sure the sword will be there,' Dirk said.

'I know it is there!' Alimud Din cried confidently.

'You don't understand,' Jim broke in impatiently. 'Your story is a *legend*. No doubt there was a Spaniard called Don Carlos

Legaspi. He might even have jumped into the Sacred Well to escape capture, but his sword held no fabulous secret!'

'It was not Don Carlos's sword, it was the Sword of Cordovada,' Alimud Din replied simply, but with a touch of resentment. 'It will bring fortune to the man who claims it.'

Jim shook his head. 'If there ever was such a sword it must have rusted away after two centuries at the bottom of a well.'

Alimud Din's face set stubbornly. 'Señor, I have seen the sword at the bottom of the Sacred Well in a dream. Three times—' and the Moro held up three fingers in emphasis – 'three times I have dreamed this same dream, and I have seen the sword. It is but two feet in length, has a gold-inlaid hilt, and is encased in an ivory scabbard. It lies in the sand at the bottom of the well. It is proof to me, descendant of the Minganoro sultans, when Allah sends me these dreams, that my fortune is linked with the Sword of Cordovada. Fate cast your captain upon the reef so that I should rescue him, and that he in his turn should retrieve the sword for me.'

Jim exchanged glances with Dirk, who had been listening intently. This confession of a dream, three dreams in fact, associated with a story which in itself was only a fable, seemed to confirm that Alimud Din was determined to believe only what he wanted to believe.

The Moro turned to Dirk again. 'Señor Rogers, I have your promise, and you are a man of honour. The Sacred Well of Kala Valley lies but two miles from the sea-shore. There is a trail from a cove beyond Jalna village, a trail I have travelled scores of times since I was a boy to look into the well waters, hoping some day a miracle would give me the sword. Señor, this north-east wind will carry us to that cove in one hour. In less than another hour we can reach the well, and in one hour more we will be on our way back *with the sword!*'

Alimud Din stared at Dirk heavily and pleadingly, and there was a moment's pregnant silence between them. Then the young pearling master said, 'Let's make ready, the sooner we start the sooner we will get back!'

In an instant the Moro's face was happy with smiles. 'A

thousand thanks, señor! Allah will reward you with an honourable old age.'

Jim turned dubiously to his skipper. 'If that's your decision, Dirk, I'd better come along too. A hundred-and-seventy-foot dive is a deep one, even down a well.'

But Alimud Din broke in quickly. 'That will not be necessary, or even wise, my friend, for in my dream I saw but one man retrieve the sword. Surely it would be tempting the Fates for another to come with us. Besides, Señor Jim, you will not wish to leave your boat here with just three simple sailors and a valuable cargo of pearl-shell. Tawan is full of thieves and robbers. I would not want to be responsible for any trouble that befell my good friends.'

'There's sound sense in what he says,' Dirk agreed before Jim could protest. 'We don't want to leave the boat without anybody in charge. Besides, there's the foremast rigging to finish, and if possible I'd like us to get under way tomorrow, Jim.' He turned to speak directly to Alimud Din. 'Bring your vinta alongside. I'll get what gear I need and we'll start at once. There's just one condition,' he added warningly and finally. 'I will make only one dive. If I find nothing, then we must return empty-handed and with no complaints. Is that understood?'

'You will need but one dive,' the Moro said emphatically.

Alimud Din wisely did not stay to discuss any further problems. His object achieved he left the cabin as though he had wings on his feet. Dirk and Jim followed him on deck into the breezy sunshine which made Tawan look as bright and gay as a picture postcard.

'I'll take a double tank and I'll use a shotrope for the dive,' Dirk said. 'I'd better have a hand-lamp too. It will be dark at the bottom of that well, even if the water's clear.'

A twin set of yellow-painted air tanks was brought from the diving locker to be charged by the motor air-compressor on deck. By the time Alimud Din paddled his vinta alongside the *Jolo* Dirk had all his gear ready. Besides his tanks and usual diving equipment he was taking with him an underwater hand-lamp and a thirty-fathom line to use as a shotrope.

The gear was soon stowed aboard the vinta, then watched by the

Jolo's crew Dirk joined Alimud Din and together they paddled the light craft away from the schooner. At the harbour mouth they hoisted sail, tacked to clear the outer reef, then set a southerly course down the coast.

Conditions were ideal for vinta sailing, with a light following breeze that kept the vessel speeding over the swell like a sleigh on blue ice. There was no need to beat out to sea. They held a course roughly a mile off shore, passed close under the forested steeps of Harun Head and soon, within the hour, drew abreast of Jalna village. The seascape was deserted except for the glimpse of a big freighter hull down on the horizon. A few gulls kept the vinta company, and once Dirk's roving eye sighted the blanket shape of a great manta ray sunning its brown white-spotted bulk on the surface.

Two miles beyond Jalna they rounded a rocky point and stood towards a cove of golden sand backed by a steep hillside thick with jungle. They jumped overboard in the shallows and manhandled their craft through the surf, dragging it clear of the tide and making it fast with a grapnel.

Dirk stood with his back to the sea, hands on hips, surveying the situation. Here in this wild cove they were as alone as men could ever be. The jungle billowed green on the hill-side, falling steeply to the palm-fringed beach. At their backs the apple-green shallows deepened into the blue of the Gulf.

Without wasting any more time they unloaded their equipment. Dirk had his diving gear and a haversack packed with food, coffee, a first-aid kit and an electric torch. Alimud Din had brought nothing but a thirty-foot rope-ladder with bamboo rungs. Well lashed though it was it made a considerable burden in itself.

'What's the ladder for?' Dirk demanded.

'You will see when we reach the Sacred Well,' Alimud Din replied cryptically, mellowing the remark with a cheerful grin. The Moro was wearing a white tunic, shorts and sandals and a red fez. In a blue sash about his waist he carried a bolo, a heavy knife some twelve inches in length.

They divided their equipment into two loads and Alimud Din

led the way along the beach to a point where an overgrown trail led
up the hill-side. After a tough zigzag climb, which lasted almost half
an hour, they reached the crest of the hill where they rested for a
while. Then, taking up their loads once more, they struck off
through waist-high grass, with the tough Moro again taking the
lead, eventually entering a green dripping gorge where the breeze
was lost in the tree-tops. Dirk was glad when they emerged from
this breathless fetid ravine into open country once more.

Alimud Din had come to a halt, and he pointed ahead to a
strange landscape. 'This is Kala Valley, señor. We have not far to
go.'

'Thank heaven for that,' Dirk remarked, brushing sweat from his
brow.

This was not a valley in the normal sense but rather a steep-sided
dry gulf. It seemed as though a solid block of the plateau, two or
three miles long and about a quarter of a mile in width, had at some
primeval time suddenly subsided for two hundred feet. The valley
floor was walled in by cliffs, and it consisted of dry, flat grassland,
occasional clumps of jungle and stretches of naked rock.

Already Alimud Din was plodding on, eager to reach their
journey's end, and the faint trail he followed skirted deep rock holes
or pits, festooned with creepers and flowering shrubs, where Dirk
caught the gleam of cool water.

'This is a valley of many natural springs,' Alimud Din explained
briefly as he paused once for Dirk to draw abreast of him.

They carried on for a while longer until they came within view of
a curious dome of cracked limestone rock. Here Alimud Din called
a halt and they set down their loads. The Moro signalled for Dirk to
follow him on to the bare limestone dome to the edge of a jagged
hole.

This hole in the middle of the dome was some eighteen feet in
diameter, and when Dirk knelt down on its edge he gazed into one
of the most sinister places he'd ever seen. The dome was the ceiling
of a huge chamber above a natural well – and the surface of this well
was almost thirty feet below the stone roof. Now Dirk realised why
Alimud Din had brought the rope-ladder. He would need it to

reach the water and, on his return, to climb back to the hole in the roof.

The pearler skipper had heard of such places before. In Yucatan they were known as cenotes. The floor of Kala Valley must consist of porous limestone honeycombed through the ages by subterranean streams into all sorts of passages and caverns.

'This is the Sacred Well,' Alimud Din confirmed in a hoarse whisper, and he looked into Dirk's grim bronzed face a little apprehensively, as though fearing the young diver would raise some last-minute objection to their pact.

'I'm beginning to understand why nobody followed Don Carlos Legaspi down there,' Dirk said feelingly. 'You say it's twenty-eight fathoms deep?'

'I have plumbed it with a weighted line many times, señor. Within a foot or so it is twenty-eight fathoms – not including the distance to the water of course.'

'What is that noise I hear below?' Dirk demanded, turning his head to listen acutely.

'Only bats,' Alimud Din responded mildly.

Dirk could hear a weird hiss and rustle of life somewhere beneath the roof they were kneeling on, but there was nothing to fear from bats, so he began his preparations and directed the eager Moro what to do.

First they found an adequate stone to weight Dirk's shotrope, or descending line, which they anchored to a small tree growing near the well. The weighted rope was passed into the well and it descended just about dead centre. Dirk ran it over a bough wedged between rocks to guard against its being cut on the edge. He checked the amount of line run out, and when the weighted end touched bottom he discovered that Alimud Din's estimate of twenty-eight fathoms was correct.

Now Dirk slipped off his clothes and put on the diving trunks he had brought in his haversack. He buckled on the twin air tanks and a weighted belt, with a sheathed knife attached, and he drew on his swimfins. He strapped on a depth gauge, compass and underwater wrist-watch, then looped the strap of his pressurised hand-lamp over his head so that the lamp rested on his chest. He adjusted his divemask and then, as grotesque a figure as had ever been seen in Kala Valley, he walked to the edge of the Sacred Well.

Meanwhile Alimud Din had been busy fixing his rope-ladder into position so that it extended from the hole in the cavern roof down to water level. Dirk had directed the Moro to secure a stone sinker to the bottom rung of the ladder, and he meant to use this sinker to speed his descent. At the edge he suddenly held a warning finger under the Moro's nose. 'One dive, Alimud, and we call it a day! That's agreed?'

'One dive, señor! All is well. Allah be with you. You are a brave and noble man!'

Without disheartening himself further by studying the thirty-foot drop into the well, Dirk got on to his knees and lowered himself over the edge. He did not bother using the ladder going down, although he would need it to ascend, and he simply lowered himself hand under hand until he reached the water. It was warm and he came to rest shoulder deep, slipping one arm over a ladder rung to support himself. Looking up he could see bright blue sky framed rudely by the jagged hole, with Alimud Din's fez-topped avid face poised on the edge like a theatrical mask.

Dirk's intrusion had triggered a screaming commotion among the scores of black bats roosting beneath the cavern roof, but their alarm soon evaporated and they subsided into their former rustling squeaking semi-quietude.

Now Dirk gripped his mouthpiece, turned on his air and began to breathe from his tanks. He unfastened the stone sinker from the ladder and slipped a wrist through the rope loop attached to it. This sinker would carry him smoothly and quickly to the bottom. His laden tanks, weights and other equipment gave him a negative buoyancy and he could have swum down, head foremost, but that would have been a waste of both energy and time.

He shifted his grip to the shotrope, then allowed himself to sink a foot under water where he tested his valves. The exhaust bubbles from the regulator on top of his air tanks gurgled gently on the surface of the usually silent pool.

Thirty feet overhead Alimud Din lay looking over the lip of the cavern roof. He could see air bubbles breaking surface and under them the diver's distorted outline and the glimmer of his yellow tanks. Then the indistinct shape began to sink fairly rapidly, fathom after fathom, into the still waters of the well, but it remained visible for a long time like a gnomish movement far, far below.

Chapter Five

Black Depths

Dirk always made a point of descending as quickly as possible, within the limits of comfort and safety. The stone he had chosen was just weighty enough to carry him down smoothly; but every few fathoms he checked his descent on the shotrope, which was running through the crook of his right arm, for his body needed time to adjust itself to the increasing pressure of air which he drew through his demand valve, via a reducing valve, from the ton-per-inch pressure of his tanks.

The well was crystal clear and he could see grey rock walls slipping past him like the track of a grotesque film. Occasionally he saw fish – blue-black creatures with large heads about six inches in length. The water was warm and pleasant until he had descended ten fathoms, then suddenly he crashed through a thermocline – a level where warm and cold waters meet. The temperature was frigid by comparison and the sudden coldness momentarily stopped his breathing so that he was forced to check his descent on the shotrope to recover.

The well was gradually narrowing but it retained its roughly circular shape. It was like descending an immensely long funnel. The water colour deepened to a smoky green which shaded slowly to a bluish hue, then finally and quite abruptly became an inky gloom.

Once again Dirk checked his descent and looked up. The surface showed as a remote patch of light, like a silver plate. He allowed himself to continue in his slow fall; then after another fathom or so he touched bottom. He switched on his lamp and, on the instant, as the beam threw a golden glow back from the bottom walls of the well, he felt a living movement!

A muscular body had touched his leg. Then he glimpsed a sinuous creature hugging the sandy floor as it vanished into the darkness of a large crevice. It was an eel, a big one, about four feet long.

Dirk began moving his lamp beam around to get his bearings, and he discovered two crevices, opposite each other, in an east–west line over the well floor. The westerly crevice was wide but less than eighteen inches high; the easterly opening was the height of a man and some three feet in width. In there his lamplight stabbed through darkness for some ten feet, then faded, smothered by the blackness beyond.

The floor of the well was composed of fine-grained sand, and in places rocks protruded, possibly fragments of the collapsed roof which had plunged to the bottom millenniums ago.

As he carefully reconnoitred his situation Dirk noticed a slight drift of sand particles in the line of the crevices from east to west, and he realised that a gentle current was flowing through some subterranean passage which linked this system of cenotes in the Kala Valley.

Methodically the pearler skipper directed his lamp beam over the sandy floor and then his searching eyes narrowed behind the glass of his divemask, and he experienced a shock of eerie discovery. His questing light had rested on the half-exposed remnants of a human skull!

He drew his knife and carefully began to scrape in the adjacent sand. He exposed more bones. A man's skeleton was lying there. Then another object came into view and the young diver levered one end from the concealing sand. Fascinatedly he drew out a two-foot-long object. It was yellowed with age and it had a corroded chain attached. It was a scabbard, and from its end protruded the blackened hilt of a sword! Alimud Din's tale was no fantasy at all but stark wonderful fact.

Dirk waited no longer. With a thrill of achievement he thrust the aged scabbard through his belt and began to rise, going hand over hand up the shotrope towards the pale orb of sunlight far above him.

He took time in ascending, for though he had been no more than a few minutes at the bottom of the cenote, and consequently there was little chance of an attack of 'bends', he dared take no risks for there was no special equipment or attention at hand if anything went wrong.

With relief he passed through the thermocline into the warm waters of the surface levels. Just a fathom deep he rested for some minutes, then at last he broke surface and gripped a rung of Alimud Din's rope-ladder.

At once he heard the Moro's excited voice. 'Señor, the sword! Have you got the sword?'

Dirk took out his mouthpiece, pushed up his divemask and gazed upwards into Alimud Din's face peering tensely over the edge of the roof.

'The sword, señor! Have you got the sword?'

Dirk hauled himself clear of the water, hooking an arm over a ladder rung. He slapped his free hand against the sword and scabbard thrust into his belt.

'I have it here,' he cried with a grin.

Alimud Din let out a choking cry of triumph. 'Allah be praised! Oh, you are a noble man! What a brave man! What a diver!'

Dirk went up the side of the rope-ladder, hand over hand, until he was within arm's reach of the roof edge.

'Give me a lift over the edge, Alimud. This gear is quite a load!'

'First pass me the sword, señor,' the Moro cried apprehensively. 'For Allah's sake let us have it safe and sound. You might lose it from your belt as you come over the edge. You will not dive again for it, and such a cursed tragedy is unthinkable! Please pass me the sword!'

It was the obvious thing to do because the sword and scabbard made an awkward accessory to all Dirk's equipment, so he drew the ancient discoloured scabbard and sword from his belt and passed them into the Moro's eager clutching hands.

'One moment, let me first put it in a safe place,' Alimud Din said feverishly. He disappeared from the roof edge with the sword. A moment passed, then the rope-ladder gave way and Dirk went hurtling downwards to land with a tremendous splash in the well. He sank a fathom deep and saw white water flashing past his eyes. Gasping for breath he came to the surface.

He trod water for a moment or two, bewildered and wondering what had happened. Then, seeing the shotrope still suspended over the roof edge, he caught hold of it and put his weight on it. As he did so it gave way and he sank again. In another moment he was back on the surface, now not only bewildered but deeply alarmed. The rope-ladder was floating beside him, buoyed by its bamboo rungs, and the free end of the shotrope was lying over it.

'Alimud!' Dirk's voice echoed resonantly in the bell-like cavern. All around him bats were whirling and shrieking, and the water was still lapping noisily after his weighty fall. Suddenly the Moro's face appeared over the roof edge. It was a savage, evil face.

'Señor, you must die! You must die!' the treacherous fellow half screamed. 'Only one man may have the Sword of Cordovada and that man is Alimud Din of the Minganoro Moros. You are a fool, Señor Rogers, and now for your folly you must die. I shall be long gone on the track of my fortune even before you are missed. And if your friend should ever find you, señor, it will be at the bottom of the well!'

With this fierce threat Alimud Din vanished. Dirk had made no reply, and he did not attempt to call the man back, for in this bitter moment he recognised how completely he had been used and fooled by the traitorous Moro, and he knew the futility of asking mercy from a merciless heart. He was left alone in the quietening pool with the grim knowledge of how he had been duped. Alimud Din had obviously never meant him to leave this place alive, no doubt because he believed that one man alone, himself, should have possession and possibly even knowledge of the sword.

Dirk was still treading water and of course he carried all his diving gear. His mouthpiece floated on his chest and his divemask was pushed up on his forehead. He had not used much of his air,

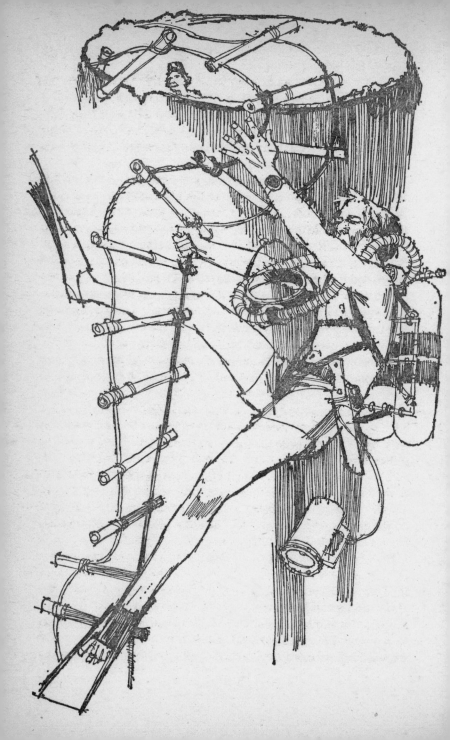

only a part of one tank, and his tanks were still heavy, increasing his tendency to submerge when he stopped treading water. His hands moved to his weighted belt to cast it adrift, then he checked the impulse. He needed time to think before he took any sort of decisive action, so he swam to the rock wall, gripped a ledge and considered his situation.

He was soon dismally assured that he would never get out of the place without assistance. Rock ledges only offered handholds close to the water and from there the domed cavern roof curved upwards to the central hole thirty feet overhead. Only bats could get out of the Sacred Well. If Alimud Din had locked him in a castle dungeon he could not have put him in a more formidable prison.

Dirk's only hope of survival appeared to be to wait for rescue, and there were only two ways of waiting. He could throw off his gear and possible find some nook or cranny where he might lodge himself, or he could siphon the air from his tanks and use them as a raft to stay afloat in the well. But the chances were that rescue might never come at all. Jim wouldn't even get anxious until nightfall, and when he did begin a search he wouldn't know where to look.

As he rested there, gripping the ledge, Dirk's gaze fell on the floating ladder from which suspended the severed end of the shotrope, and suddenly a startling possibility occurred to him.

The Sacred Well was only one of several such places in Kala Valley. Possibly it was the biggest, deepest and most inaccessible from the surface, but it must be linked with others. A current flowed through caverns below. And there was the eel! There must be an exit because eels couldn't breed in a closed well. Was the passage used by eels big enough for a man – a diver?

Dirk checked his air gauge and noted he'd used only one quarter of one tank. He estimated he could reach the well bottom, spend fifteen minutes exploring and, if there was no way out below, still have sufficient air left to return to the surface. There was the problem of getting quickly to the bottom, for he'd left his sinker on the well floor and to swim down would take a lot of energy and a lot of air which had become vitally precious. The shotrope, hanging over the partially submerged runged ladder, presented a way around this problem. There was a stone sinker on the end of that rope which he could use to warp himself down.

Dirk cast another look up at the sky. Just for a moment he wondered if he should take the chance. Then he drew down his divemask, blew the water out of his mouthpiece and gripped it between his teeth. Breathing from his tanks he swam to the shotrope, dived and took hold of it, hauling it in until it drew taut. Kicking his fins he began to warp himself down by the line, hand over hand.

The task needed no effort for his gear still gave him negative buoyancy. He breathed shallowly to conserve his air and increase his downward momentum. It was a familiar plunge through the green upper waters down to the blue fog beneath, and through the thermocline into the inky icy gloom of the lower levels. The sloping walls of the rock shaft closed about him and at last, for the second time, he drew himself down on his knees to the sandy floor.

As he did so he felt something coiling about his shoulders. He flinched, thinking of the eel, then he realised it was the shotrope freed from the floating ladder on the surface, slowly sinking and falling upon him. The circumstance provoked another idea, and he began hauling the rope down quickly. When he came to the end of it he made it fast to his belt. It would serve as a guide line back to the well if he should find himself in some dead-end tunnel.

Dirk switched on his lamp and moved the beam around the well bottom. He had already decided to take the crevice eastwards, leading high up the valley, for he remembered the steep hill-side on the coast, and he guessed any passages leading that way would end in pits, gullies and waterfalls.

His underwater lamp sent a fuzzy glow creeping ahead as he entered the crevice he had chosen. He found himself in a smooth-walled tunnel where his air exhaust made such an unexpected roar he imagined for a moment he was approaching a cataract; but the black water remained uncannily still.

Soon his light reflected from solid stone ahead and he had to feel his way around a rock obstruction till he found another tunnel.

Now as he swam on slowly the roof began lowering on him and he wondered if he were swimming into a bottle-neck from which he couldn't get back. He looked at his luminous watch. His time from the surface on this second trip was still less than ten minutes, but it had seemed like ten hours.

Abruptly the roof began rising again, floor and walls vanished out of his light beam and he realised he had entered a submerged cavern, how big he couldn't even guess. He was having difficulty with his guide line, which he was hauling after him. It was riding over rocks behind him, and when he tugged on it he had a tendency to drag himself backwards. At length, when he was beginning to feel he must return, his lamp again illuminated the roof. It was descending again ahead of him and with groping hands he followed it down, steadily down to a sandy floor and a further low crevice.

Suddenly Dirk experienced a strange giddiness. When it passed he rested on his knees and looked at his depth gauge. He was forty fathoms deep – *two hundred and forty feet!*

This knowledge of his great depth sapped Dirk's courage. Instead of finding a way out he was going deeper. He was also getting near the point of no return as far as his air was concerned, for he was working on his second tank. Just for a moment, alone, abandoned and lost in the freezing silence of the watery catacomb, he grappled with a wave of despair. But the moment passed and with a kind of herculean determination he decided to give himself five more minutes before he started tracing his guide line back. So he entered the crevice.

Almost at once the roof began to rise and he followed it upwards. He found himself in a narrow shaft where he could touch the rock sides on either hand. The shaft widened and he ascended steadily. At length he switched out his lamp. The water was no longer black, it was a grey ghostly hue, and when he looked up he saw far above him a strangely disturbed whitish surface.

It was at this moment he felt his ascent checked by the line he was trailing. This time he could not get an inch of slack on it for it had run out to the bitter end. But there was no choice to make now, for even if he did go back to the Sacred Well he knew he wouldn't have enough air – enough to reach the surface perhaps, but he needed more than that, for he had been fifteen minutes submerged at depths reaching forty fathoms. He needed at least thirty minutes of air to decompress near the surface otherwise he would probably collapse with an attack of the 'bends'.

His numbed fingers tugged at the guide line and he cast it loose. Then, lifted by his light tanks – they were losing a pound weight with every sixteen cubic feet of air he used – he rose towards that distant frothy surface. Minutes passed, the water changed from grey to light green, and then above the whistles of his own exhaust bubbles he heard a diffused dull thrashing sound.

He was back in warmer water and his shivering limbs felt the wonderful benefit of it. At forty feet deep he gripped a ledge on the shaft side and checked his gauges. He was on the last half of his second tank but there was enough air for him to decompress if all went well.

After a five-minute decompression he decided to risk the 'bends' for a glimpse of what awaited him on the surface. He started upwards again and soon he was immersed in turbulent water that clouded his divemask. He broke surface under a downpour and for some moments he was too bewildered to understand where he was. Then he struggled into clear water, pushed up his divemask and discovered he had emerged beneath a small waterfall.

He was in a long gully under a cliff edge some forty feet high . . . but on the farther side there was a shelf of rock which rose into a low bank-side covered with ferns, and with a shiver of relief he knew he would be able to get out.

But he still had to go down into that grim water once more, otherwise he would no sooner reach dry land than the nitrogen dissolved in his blood-stream under pressure would begin to emerge as gas bubbles to cripple him with the 'bends'.

He dived again, but this time in good heart. At fifteen feet deep he found an overhang where he stayed until he went over to his last 'reserve' and when his breathing grew 'hard' he knew the second tank was almost finished. He surfaced, exhaling steadily all the time.

Dirk swam towards the rock shelf where green weed swayed in clouds, and he dragged himself ashore. There he lay in the late afternoon sunshine with the breeze drumming musically in the ferns about him. It was many minutes later before he sat up and slowly and painfully removed his gear. When he stood up his legs felt like rubber; but he was tough and fit and he soon recovered.

Carrying his gear with him he struggled through a welter of undergrowth to the top of the bank and, although he should have expected it, he could scarcely believe his eyes when he saw the domed contour of the Sacred Well about thirty yards away. It seemed incredible that he'd spent a black eternity covering a distance that seemed only a step in the open air.

When he reached the place where earlier he had undressed and put on his diving gear he was astonished to find his haversack, his neat bundle of clothes and his shoes still in the cleft where he had left them. Alimud Din must have been made witless by his possession of the sword. He could so easily have thrown all evidence of Dirk into the well, but he hadn't bothered or cared.

Dirk dressed himself and he found a welcome flask of coffee and a sandwich in the haversack. Then, feeling thoroughly able again, he set off for the coast.

Chapter Six

On to Port Balacon

It was dark, an hour after sunset, when Miguel Gomez, overseer of the Jalna timber station, heard footsteps approaching on the path from the jungle, and then a knock on his door. He was startled, because he knew his workers had all gone home, and this was a lonely place at night. He was working late in his ramshackle office in front of a window covered by a bamboo blind. A large-two bladed fan squeaked monotonously as it turned the humid air in the office. Gomez laid down his pen and cautiously opened the office door.

'Señor Rogers!' he exclaimed, for the tall figure of the pearler skipper was standing on his doorstep. 'What on earth brings you here at this time of night? Come inside, my friend, you look tired.'

Dirk unshouldered the burden of his diving gear and set it in a corner of the office, then he gladly dropped into the chair Gomez offered him. His shirt was sweat-stained, he was tired-eyed and weary.

'I thought you had gone to Tawan. Did you not meet your partner there?' Gomez inquired wonderingly.

'It's quite a story what happened to me today,' Dirk said. 'Before I tell you about it can you please put a radio call through to Tawan and have someone take a message to my partner?'

'I think so, señor, but of course you must stay with me tonight. We will go to my bungalow where you can rest, then I will have your message sent from the coastguard station.'

'That's real kind of you,' Dirk said gratefully.

Twenty minutes later both men were sitting down to a meal

prepared by Gomez's Chinese cook. Gomez had succeeded in having a radio message dispatched to Tawan with a request that Jim Cartwright should be informed that Dirk would arrive on the following morning.

'I am curious to know what has happened today,' Gomez told his visitor. 'I have a suspicion your tale is concerned with Alimud Din.'

Dirk relaxed in his chair and began to relate exactly what had occurred since he had last seen Gomez. The overseer listened without interruption and the tale, which Dirk did not elaborate, was soon told.

'When I got back to the Sacred Well and discovered Alimud Din had left my clothes there I collected my gear and made my way down to the coast,' the pearler skipper said finally. 'I knew it was no use going back to the bay where we'd landed, so I kept along the plateau edge till I found a trail leading to Jalna village. I didn't want to go marching into the datu's house without making some inquiries first, so I skirted the village and came calling on you.'

They had finished eating and were talking over their coffee. Gomez was smoking a strong black cheroot. He smoothed his thin black moustache with a crooked forefinger and his shrewd face was full of wonder at Dirk's story.

'Señor, you are a man with many lives! What a fabulous escape!' he declared in an awed whisper. 'Myself, I have never heard tell of this legend of Cordovada's Sword, but truly it explains all of Alimud Din's strange talk. And it is a fact that you recovered this ancient sword from the bottom of the Sacred Well!'

'Just as Alimud Din predicted I would,' Dirk said.

'The black-hearted dog!' Gomez exclaimed softly. 'I guessed he was a little mad but I did not suppose he had such foul treachery in him. He is a danger to honest men and a grief to his old father. But you will not find him at Jalna, señor.'

'What do you know of his movements?' Dirk asked.

Gomez shrugged his thin shoulders. 'The datu and I are old friends and I visit him almost every day. Tonight I found him grief-stricken.'

'What had happened?'

'It seems that Alimud Din sailed his vinta into the creek about four o'clock today. He paid a lightning visit to his father's house and left at once, telling no one where he was bound. When he had gone the datu discovered that his son had made off with two valuable muskets, heirlooms of the family, the personal weapons of the last ruling sultan of the Minganoro Moros.'

'What would Alimud Din want with muskets?' Dirk asked.

'He must have needed money,' Gomez said without hesitation. 'The datu had several times been offered a good price for those antique muskets but he would never sell. Alimud Din must have wanted to raise some cash.'

'It seems he doesn't mean to return.'

'He will not return. He would not dare face his father's wrath.'

'Maybe you're right,' Dirk said. 'Anyhow I won't upset the old man any more by telling him what Alimud Din did to me. But I'd have liked to know why his son wanted that sword so desperately.'

'It is a mystery indeed,' Gomez replied, 'and no one can say for sure where Alimud Din has gone, but I think I can make a good guess. There is a dealer at Port Balacon forty miles higher up the coast. He is an Irishman, and his name is Patrick O'Hara. He buys all sorts of antique stuff and sells it again in Davao, where it finds its way into the hands of tourists, collectors and buyers for museums.'

'So you think Alimud Din will have gone to this Irish dealer,' Dirk commented.

'For three reasons, señor. Firstly because he already knows the man as we all do at Jalna, secondly because it is not too far to travel in his vinta, and thirdly because O'Hara will ask no questions if he can make a good bargain.'

'Port Balacon,' Dirk murmured. 'Jim and I could well sell our pearl-shell there instead of going on to Davao.'

'If you decide to visit Patrick O'Hara do not forget to mention my name. He knows me well,' Gomez said.

Dirk did not sleep well that night. He shared Gomez's only bedroom and as he lay beneath the mosquito-net on a narrow bed he had bad confused dreams about Alimud Din, the ancient Sword of Cordovada and the black tunnels and caverns beneath the floor of Kala Valley.

He awakened in the middle of the night to hear rain thundering on the bungalow roof and a wild squall of wind wailing in the near-by palms. The room was lit by a yellow glow, and for an instant he thought Alimud Din's evil face was glowering over him.

Then he realised that someone was really there, not Alimud Din – but Gomez! The overseer had drawn aside the mosquito-net. He was holding an oil-lamp and was staring down at the young skipper with a rapt expression on his sharp-featured face.

'What's wrong?' Dirk demanded warily.

'Nothing is wrong, but I could not sleep because I must tell you of my decision,' Gomez whispered in a voice that trembled with anticipation. 'Señor, I am lying awake thinking about the Sword of Cordovada. Did not Alimud Din see it in a dream at the bottom of the Sacred Well? And it was there, Señor Rogers – you found it, and you gave it into his hands, the very sword brought across the ocean two centuries ago by Don Carlos Legaspi whose story is written in the Arabic scripts.'

'I told you that before we came to bed,' Dirk said wonderingly.

'The mystery of it, the wonder of it is only now apparent to me,' Gomez declared. 'I ask myself what sort of a man I am to be cutting lumber and writing up accounts when this piece of fate is crossing my path. Señor Rogers, I feel in my bones that Alimud Din will have gone to Patrick O'Hara, the Irishman who deals in everything at Port Balacon. The villain will have gone to sell the loot he stole from his father's house, and he will have the Sword of Cordovada with him!'

'What of it?' Dirk asked.

'What of it? You can lie there and say that, Señor Rogers? Are we not speaking of fate and fortune? A man is lucky if he gets one chance in a lifetime to follow such a path of adventure. May I be spit upon by both the endless lines of my family for a spineless dullard if I stay behind. I will go with you to Patrick O'Hara.'

'I don't know if I'm going to Port Balacon. I've got to talk to my partner first. We've a cargo of pearl-shell to sell and a living to make.'

'Of course we must go to Port Balacon! Already Alimud Din has twenty-four hours' start. We can sleep no more this night until you promise,' Gomez hissed vehemently.

'What about your job? How can you leave it?'

'Señor, I have an assistant who is just waiting to step into my shoes and will be delighted to see me go. Moreover, I can find a similar job at any time. I am an excellent overseer. Do not concern yourself with my job. I have enough money saved to pay my way.'

'Let's think about it in the morning,' Dirk suggested.

'No, no, señor, these things cannot be thought about in the morning, for then we would no doubt have changed our minds.'

Dirk sighed helplessly. The rain was still thrashing on the roof and the wind was buffeting the window-shutters and making an uproar in the jungle. He was very tired and he couldn't be bothered to argue.

'Very well, Gomez. We'll go to Port Balacon and see O'Hara. I suppose it's as good a place as any other.'

Morning came, still windy, with low bruised cloudbanks sweeping across the Gulf over a white-flecked pounding sea. Dirk had hoped Gomez would think differently in daylight, but his hopes were futile. The little overseer's excitement had simply resolved into a stubborn determination and, after an early breakfast, they were soon ready to leave. Gomez had written letters, given instructions to his assistant, and packed his bag. On the weed-grown jetty they said a brief goodbye to the staff then, with Dirk carrying his diving gear, they boarded the timber station's cargo launch.

The launch was a thirty-year-old barge-like craft powered by a crank diesel engine which seemed as though its primary function was to shake the weatherbeaten hull to pieces.

It was a wet squally trip to Tawan that morning. The trip took longer than it had done in Alimud Din's vinta and when Dirk and Gomez stepped ashore on the sea wall at Tawan it was nearly midday and the weather was changing. The sun was eating up the

clouds, the wind was dying and it was growing very hot. Jim was waiting and he was surprised to find they were to have company when Miguel Gomez was introduced to him.

'Señor Rogers, I have relatives in the town – four brothers, two sisters and my wife and five children—' Gomez started to explain.

'Your wife and five children,' Dirk interrupted in astonishment. 'I didn't even know you were married.'

'The matter slipped my mind,' Gomez said with a grin. 'I will say goodbye to them and keep out of the way while you inform your partner of our plans. My family will be well cared for while I am gone by my brothers and sisters.'

Gomez shifted his gaze to the smooth muddy waters of the inner harbour where the *Jolo* was lying alongside a jetty. The schooner was practically ready for sea, with her new rigging set up and her bulwarks repaired.

'I see your boat there, Señor Rogers. She is a nice craft. It will be a pleasure to sail in her.'

With this remark the little overseer hurried off with his canvas bag of meagre belongings, and Jim stared after him curiously.

'What plans is he talking about?' he inquired doubtfully of Dirk.

'Gomez is only a small part of the yarn I have to tell you, Jim,' the pearler skipper answered. 'Let's go below and have a talk.'

The tide was full, lapping gently at the sun-dried jetty timbers, and the *Jolo* heaved a little as they stepped down from her bulwarks on to the foredeck. They went below to the saloon cabin. Here the ship's cook had a meal waiting and, as they ate, Dirk told his partner all that had occurred since he'd embarked on his venture to the Sacred Well with Alimud Din.

'That was a tough experience, Dirk. Seems like you've used up two lives already this trip!' Jim said when the story was finished. 'And now you tell me you've pledged us to go to Port Balacon and take this queer fellow Miguel Gomez with us.'

'We could do worse, Jim. Port Balacon is a lot bigger place than Tawan, a port of call for the Davao liners. We should find a buyer there for our shell and perhaps pick up a return cargo to Zamboanga. Besides,' Dirk added with a ghost of a smile, 'Gomez isn't the only one who wonders why Alimud Din wanted that sword.'

Jim nodded with an answering grin. 'I guess you're right, Dirk, and maybe this Irish dealer at Port Balacon can give us the answer,' he said.

When Miguel Gomez arrived back later that afternoon he found the *Jolo* ready to sail. The tide was on the ebb, but still high, and the schooner put to sea within the hour. She cleared the outer reefs under motor power, then hoisted sail, and on a steady wind she set a northerly course up the coast.

The sun was low over the ridge of the shadowed interior mountains when the *Jolo* rounded the South Point into Balacon Bay. The port had a good harbour, with a long T-shaped steamer pier where the Davao liners called on a regular service, and the town itself was an uneasy mixture of old and new, peopled by a potpourri of races – Moros, Filipinos, Chinese, Malays, a few Europeans and Americans and, of course, the Irish dealer, Patrick O'Hara.

The crew sat down to an evening meal as the short tropical twilight deepened. Lights were springing up along the waterfront, lanterns began to glow in the native prau harbour and cargo lamps illuminated the decks of two deep-sea freighters lying alongside the main pier.

Chapter Seven

O'Hara Remembers

It was dark when Dirk and Jim launched the ship's dinghy. Accompanied by Gomez, who was taking them to O'Hara's store, they rowed ashore over the quiet harbour waters. They tied up the dinghy at some jetty steps and Gomez led the way along the starlit waterfront. The overseer knew exactly where to go and within a few minutes they found O'Hara sitting at a table on the front porch of his white-painted store.

'Damn me eyes if it isn't Miguel Gomez! What divil from Jalna has chased ye here? But I'm delighted to see ye, man, for I'm sittin' here by meself as melancholy as a motherless pup!' The dealer delivered this greeting in a mighty brogue. He did not shout, but his natural speaking voice was so deep, round and resonant it could be heard a hundred yards away.

He had got to his feet to take Gomez's hand in his iron grip. And indeed he was the most formidable fellow in bulk and voice that either Dirk or Jim had met in many a long day. His sun-tanned body was naked to the waist, revealing the shoulders of an ox and biceps big enough for two ordinary men. He was wearing just a pair of dungarees rolled up from his shins and open sandals on his outsize feet.

'Ye've brought company too,' he declared as Gomez introduced his companions. 'Dirk Rogers and Jim Cartwright,' he repeated, apparently informing all the harbour of their identity. 'I do believe I've heard o' ye both. Ye'll be from the schooner that put into the bay this evenin'. I fell in love wid that craft as soon as I seen her round the Point. Sit down, gentlemen. Make yourselves comfortable and I'll have me assistant fetch ye some coffee for I'm about to have some meself.

'Jose!' he roared in a voice that made the store tremble. 'Jose, are ye there, lad?'

Almost at once an elderly smiling Filipino appeared from the lighted store.

'Fetch me guests some refreshment,' O'Hara requested, 'and please don't be wastin' time about it.'

As the old store assistant turned away O'Hara picked up a short yellowed pipe, put a match to it and loosed a fog of smoke into the lamplit verandah. 'I have a deal o' trouble wid Jose,' he confided in a powerful whisper. 'He's as deaf as a post and I can never hear a word he says.'

Dirk and Jim were not sure what sort of character they were confronted with, for O'Hara was a difficult man to judge on first acquaintance. His nose looked as though it had been broken years ago, and he had a scar down his right cheek, but apart from these minor disfigurements he was almost handsome, with strong features, white teeth, light blue eyes that shone like gems in his bronzed face, and black curling hair which straggled low down the nape of his solid neck and made brigandish sideboards down his hard cheeks.

'What business might be bringin' ye to Port Balacon?' he demanded of Gomez.

'Señor O'Hara, I have come with my friends for information,' Gomez said seriously, leaning his arms on the table.

'Well, it's the right man ye've come to then, for I'm so full of information I'm puttin' on weight wid the burden of it.'

Just at this moment Jose returned with a tray bearing a coffee pot and cups, and Gomez waited until the old Filipino had gone. Dirk and Jim sat silent, leaving the overseer to do the talking.

'We have come making inquiries about the son of the datu of Jalna village,' he said quietly. 'Tell us, Señor O'Hara – was Alimud Din, the Moro, here to see you?'

'He was sittin' here on my verandah only yesterday.'

Gomez sighed and glanced triumphantly at his companions. Looking again at O'Hara, he said, 'And did he try to sell you the ancient muskets which he stole from his father's house?'

'I never presumed to ask him where he stole his goods,' O'Hara answered blandly.

'We only wish to know if he sold you the muskets and where he went from here. It is very important we should know,' Gomez said.

O'Hara puffed solemnly at his pipe and his eyes shone in the half-light, very speculative and thoughtful. 'I struck a bargain wid him for his goods, and I happen to know he sold his vinta to a Chinese merchant on the waterfront, but I couldn't be sayin' *exactly* where he went from here.'

'Sold his vinta! He must really have wanted to raise some cash in a hurry,' Jim declared.

'He raised some cash out o' meself he did. I give that feller a thousand pesos for his goods,' the Irishman informed them.

'A thousand pesos for those old guns? You must have had a touch of the sun!' Gomez exclaimed.

O'Hara grinned hugely. 'Well, he told me such a pitiful yarn about his old father needin' the cash me heart was moved. I paid him five hundred pesos for the muskets and another five hundred for the sword, and I reckon I got meself quite a bargain.'

'*The sword*,' Gomez barely breathed.

Suddenly there was such a deep quiet between them that the distant sounds from the warm light-spotted harbour seemed to rush close around O'Hara's store.

'What would there be so uncommon about the sword?' the dealer asked curiously after a while. 'It was an old sword wid a gold-inlaid hilt and an ivory scabbard—'

'Not so loud, do you want to tell our business to every loafing jackal on the waterfront?' Gomez hissed.

O'Hara made a rough gesture with his pipe at the star-misted gloom of the night. 'These folk don't know what I'm talkin' about, and even if they did they wouldn't understand a word of it; but it's a feelin' I have that I've stumbled on to some kind o' mystery.' The great bare-chested fellow paused and his eyes narrowed in a hard piratical gleam.

'Indeed you have – we all have,' Gomez admitted. He laid a hand on Dirk's arm. 'Señor Rogers, I think we should tell O'Hara all we know. You must tell the story for you speak more to the point than I can.'

Dirk nodded and he looked directly at the Irish dealer who was leaning tattooed forearms on the table top, his short smouldering pipe gripped in the corner of his grim mouth.

'We were surprised to learn you had the sword in your possession, Mr O'Hara. It was the sword which brought us here, and the story I have to tell you is about the sword.'

Once again Dirk began to recount his adventures during the past few days. He told of his rescue by Alimud Din, about the legend of Don Carlos Legaspi and Alimud Din's request that he should dive for the Sword of Cordovada in the Sacred Well of Kala Valley. And as O'Hara listened with a rapt, almost childlike attention, his pipe gone out, the pearler skipper went on to describe his escape from the underground labyrinth and the events which had brought them here to the Irishman's verandah.

When Dirk had finished, O'Hara sat perfectly still for several moments as though caught up in some secret dream, his face set, and save for the beads of sweat on his brow one must have imagined he was an image beaten out of bronze.

'Do you not believe us?' Gomez whispered.

O'Hara slowly seemed to come to life. 'Oh, I believe ye, for I have a likin' for such yarns, but I wish I didn't because it can hardly be true.'

'It's all true, you have the sword to prove it,' Jim pointed out reasonably.

'That's a small point I forgot,' O'Hara murmured. 'Indeed I have the sword and I'll be proud to show it to ye if ye'll kindly step indoors.'

There was nothing any of them would have rather wished, so they eagerly followed the dealer into his store. He led them through the outer shop, which was stacked with all the variety of an Eastern ship-chandler's store, through a living-room where Jose was sitting with a cigar and a magazine, and so into an untidy rear apartment with wide open windows through which drifted the scents of a half-wild garden.

This was where O'Hara kept the antiques and curios which he collected for resale in Davao. There were weapons, vases, images, caskets and the like, enough to give the room an eerie oriental atmosphere.

'I have a nice little business here,' O'Hara told them. 'Five years I've been in Port Balacon, and with Jose and his son to help me it's been very plain sailin'. For d'ye see I've reached a time o' life when a man needs to put a bit by for the future. A rover I've been y'know, all over the Western Pacific from the Bonin Islands to the Torres Straits. It's high time I was savin' for me old age, but it sometimes worries me what a waste it will be if I don't live to enjoy it.'

As he was talking he had opened a chest on the floor and now he produced the article they all wanted to see. They gathered around the table where he laid the sword and scabbard. 'There it is,' he said, resting his fists on the table top and gazing down at the sheathed sword. 'I spent all mornin' cleanin' it.'

Dirk took the sword and scabbard in his hands. The scabbard was yellow with age, and the black sword hilt, inlaid with gold, protruded from it some seven inches.

'It is wonderfully preserved to have spent two hundred years at the bottom of a well,' Jim remarked.

'It has been protected by a covering of sand,' Dirk pointed out.

'I've been busy wid it all day and I just managed to git the sword free o' the scabbard this afternoon,' O'Hara said.

Dirk gently drew the weapon from its scabbard. It was a Spanish blade just two feet in length with a cup-like guard.

'Did you make these marks on the hilt?' Dirk asked O'Hara, indicating recent indentations above the guard.

'Oh, no, I was most careful wid the article,' the Irishman said.

'Then Alimud Din must have been at work here. Have you a pair of pliers handy, O'Hara?'

'Sure I have, but what are ye aimin' to do?'

'I want to see if the hilt will come adrift.'

O'Hara quickly reached into a near-by drawer and produced a pair of pliers which he handed to the pearler skipper. Dirk gripped the hilt and slowly twisted it in an anti-clockwise direction. It turned through ninety degrees, then he was able to withdraw it completely from the guard socket.

'See, the hilt is hollow and it has been made to lock into place with a clockwise twist,' Dirk said softly. He showed them the hilt which contained an aperture large enough to hold a fountain-pen.

'A cunning hiding-place – but there is nothing in it!' Gomez exclaimed disappointedly.

'Not now, but I think there was when it fell into Alimud Din's hands.'

'Of course, that is the answer,' Gomez agreed, taking the hilt to examine it. 'Something has been concealed here, and that cursed thief Alimud Din has discovered it. It was not the sword he wanted, but its secret!'

'Are ye sayin' the Moro found somethin' in this sword hilt?' O'Hara demanded.

Dirk nodded. 'I doubt if he would have parted with the sword unless he'd got what he wanted from it. He faithfully believed it held the key to fabulous wealth and I think he must have discovered that, in some form or another, within this secret compartment in the hilt.'

'That's a remarkable thing, indeed it is,' O'Hara muttered as he carefully fitted hilt and blade together again. 'There's somethin' else here too, this inscription, or what's left of it, on the blade.' The Irishman gathered his brows in a scowl of concentration as he laid a finger on the blade to indicate some battered embossed letters half erased by corrosion and time. 'What would ye be makin' o' that?' he inquired huskily.

Dirk intently studied the remnants of the legend. The disfigured letters read:

C . NDE AL . NSO D . COR . . VA . A MD . C . . XIV

'It seems to be the name of the sword's owner, and the date he acquired it.' Dirk said. 'I would say this inscription once read, CONDE ALONSO DE CORDOVADA. And the date, I'd guess, is 1734. Alimud Din has been right in every detail of his story. This really is the Sword of Cordovada!'

'Conde Alonso de Cordovada,' O'Hara said, lingering over the name with relish. '*Cordovada*,' he repeated. 'That's a name a man couldn't ever forget. I wonder now, I wonder whatever golden secret could have been hidden in this old sword hilt!'

As he was speaking he sat himself down at the table and almost reverently laid his hands on the sword. 'Yes, I'm askin' meself what it was that could have put such a divil into a creature like that Alimud Din for him to rob his father, sell his boat, and go chasin' over the Pacific Ocean—'

'Why d'you say that?' Jim broke in. 'We've no idea where he has gone.'

'Indeed ye haven't an idea, that's the truth, but it's meself that has,' O'Hara said with a grin. 'Chance has brought ye to the one man that might be knowin' *exactly* where that Moro has gone.'

'Did he tell you so himself?' Gomez cried.

'He told me nothin', but this name Cordovada has been knockin' in me memory ever since ye mentioned it, and when I find it written here on the sword – *why, it all comes back to me!*'

'For pity's sake, man, tell us what you are talking about!'

'There's no need for ye to get excited, just thank your lucky stars ye know an Irishman that can tell ye where to find Cordovada Island!'

'There is an island of that name?' Gomez whispered, his eyes rounding with wonder. And for some moments they were all silent, watching O'Hara's triumphant face. Then Dirk drew up a chair to the table and Gomez and Jim seated themselves on a battered sofa.

'There is such an island and I know the Moro has gone there as sure as if he'd told me himself,' O'Hara went on. 'I know he took a passage on the Davao steamer that called here yesterday, and after that vessel leaves Port Balacon it makes no stop till it reaches Koror in the Palau Islands.'

'A five-hundred-mile trip across the Western Pacific,' Dirk commented.

'Just so, man. Alimud Din must have gone to Koror because he couldn't step off that ship until he got there, and it goes no farther. Now didn't I tell ye I'd done some rovin' in me time? Well, part of it was around the Palau Islands.'

'Is that where Cordovada Island lies?' Jim asked.

'I doubt if it's marked on any chart ye have,' O'Hara said. 'There's a couple o' dozen named islands in the Palau group and scores o' unnamed uninhabited islets and atolls. Cordovada's nothin' but a big rock overgrown wid jungle, stickin' out o' the ocean wid a few reefs around it, and ye'd have to go to Kunjang, a small island farthest to the south o' the Palau group even to hear the name mentioned.

'I was out there years ago,' O'Hara went on. 'Down on me luck as usual I was, and I heard this yarn about Cordovada from the headman of Tano, a village on Kunjang. A peculiar tale it was, the sort o' weird mumbo-jumbo that would get lost in a man's mind for maybe ten years till a desperate Moro turned up wid the name on a sword!'

O'Hara broke off to laugh immensely at this sample of his humour, but there was no joke for his listeners. They were all ears to hear more of Cordovada Island.

'For mercy's sake get on with the story,' Gomez said exasperatedly.

O'Hara's brows furrowed with the effort of remembering. 'Just one night I spent in the Tano falu – that's the name they have for their All Men's House out there. I forget the headman's name, but I recall askin' him if he knew of any pearlin' ground where a man on his beam-ends might pick up a quick fortune, and he tells me there's virgin ground around Cordovada Island, two or three leagues to the south. It's virgin ground he says because the water's deep and the island's haunted, and that's why I niver went d'ye see.'

'Haunted by what?' Jim asked.

'By Cordovada himself,' O'Hara said with a ghostly smile. 'Years and years ago, it seems, back in the old-time days, when the Kunjang islanders was head-hunters, a ship was blowed to grief on this ugly rock to the south. There was a parcel o' survivors, and as soon as the Kunjang warriors heard about 'em they set off in their war canoes to collect some heads to decorate their falu. But they got a warmer reception than they'd bargained for 'cos some o' the survivors was trained fighters under the command of a feller called Cordovada.'

'The Spaniard – Conde Alonso de Cordovada!' Gomez declared.

'I reckon so,' O'Hara agreed. 'Anyhow Cordovada and his men killed half o' the head-hunters and even took a few prisoners. That was how they came to parley wid the Kunjang people.'

'What happened then?' Jim asked.

'Well, months and years went by, and the survivors just died one by one on their island till only their leader Cordovada was left. He was a great fierce feller, half mad wid despair and loneliness, and he got to be so feared that the Kunjang folk never dared land on the island. In fact if they caught sight o' him stalkin' the beach or the cliff-tops they thought it was an evil omen. No man ever knowed when or how or if he ever died, and they believe out there, to this day, that if a man sees the spectre of Cordovada he's doomed. That's why the local folk keep clear o' the island.'

'So that's the tale behind the Cordovada legend,' Dirk said when O'Hara had finished. 'He was a Spanish sea captain whose ship was cast away on a lonely island. Don Carlos Legaspi must have been one of his men who managed to get away, with Cordovada's sword, no doubt in an attempt to reach Manila and bring rescue to the remaining survivors. I wonder how much of this Alimud Din knows. What did you tell him, O'Hara?'

'I told him nothin' at all, for he never talked o' Cordovada to me. It was not until ye mentioned the name that I recalled the tale.'

'At any rate there can be no doubt that Alimud Din is on his way to Cordovada Island,' Jim said. 'How long will it take him to get out there?'

'The steamer makes Koror from here in two days,' O'Hara informed them. 'In Koror a man would need to find some local vessel to carry him south to Kunjang, and from Kunjang to Cordovada Island is no more than a longish swim.'

'But if this island is known by name only to the Kunjang people how can Alimud Din know where to find it?' Gomez demanded.

'Where would he be findin' knowledge o' Cordovada except within the hilt o' this very sword?' O'Hara stated roundly. 'I'd lay me life on it that he found some kind o' chart showin' him exactly where to go.'

'That makes sound sense,' Dirk agreed. 'And he would need to sell his father's muskets and his vinta to raise money for his expenses.'

'Then we must follow him at once! Señor Rogers, say we will go!' Gomez cried, jumping to his feet excitedly.

'It's a longish trip to the Palau Islands,' Dirk pointed out dubiously. 'Only two days' journey by the Davao liner but four or five aboard the *Jolo*, even with favourable weather. Meanwhile Jim and I have a cargo of pearl-shell to sell. Our Malay crewmen only signed for the pearling trip. They won't go to Palau.'

'Señor Rogers, we cannot give up! Are we not to know the secret of the sword? Did you dive to the bottom of the Sacred Well for nothing?'

They all looked at Dirk, who thoughtfully laid a hand on the ancient sword. 'Any man would wish to know the end of this tale and it must have an end somewhere,' he said.

'It will end where it began – on Cordovada Island,' Gomez pronounced fiercely. He turned to the silent Irishman who sat with his eyes narrowed like visor slits, his hard features set in a brooding frown. 'What about you, O'Hara?' he demanded.

'What about me?' the dealer muttered. 'Oh, man, ye're not talkin' to a child ye're not. I'm finished wid wildcat venturin'. Haven't I told ye I'm settled down here to save for me old age?'

'You were not born to be old, you great ox!' Gomez cried. 'Here's this famous sword come to your hands as if Alonso de Cordovada had sent it himself and you wish to sit in a chair on your verandah like an old woman when there's a chance for you to be as rich as a king!'

'What can the sword have to do wid makin' O'Hara rich?'

'This sword held the key to a treasure. What other explanation can there be? There is treasure on Cordovada Island. It's as plain as the nose on your face!'

'Ye're temptin' me somethin' powerful ye are,' O'Hara growled, 'for I'd like fine to feel the deck o' that little schooner under me feet. It's a longin' wid me to get back to sea, like a thirst it is.'

'If you go with us we could pay off the Malays and we would need no extra hands,' Jim pointed out.

'It's right ye are,' O'Hara agreed as the idea warmed his heart. 'And o' course Jose and his son could manage me store, and as for your cargo o' shell, Li Yen the merchant would give ye a fair price, and we could unload it first thing in the mornin'. I reckon we could be off by midday wid stores aboard and all found, and lay our course direct for Kunjang. Wid a bit o' luck we might even get to Cordovada Island before Alimud Din!'

'Now, Señor Rogers, it is up to you!' Gomez said pleadingly.

Dirk didn't take long to make up his mind. 'I reckon I was bound for Cordovada Island from the moment Alimud Din hauled me off that reef,' he said candidly. 'We'll sail for Kunjang and find out what lies in store for us there.'

O'Hara came out on to the verandah to say good night, and long after they had left his store they could hear his powerful voice talking to Jose, his assistant. A white moon was rising over Davao Gulf and Port Balacon looked like a Chinese painting, motionless in a silver quietude. The town was asleep as Dirk and his companions cast off in their dinghy, and the sound of their oars carried far across the silent harbour.

Morning came, very warm, with a nor'westerly breeze. The low hills surrounding the bay showed a vivid green against a cloudless sky. The *Jolo*'s crew were astir at daybreak and straight after breakfast they moved the schooner alongside a jetty in the prau harbour. Dirk had just completed paying off the Malay sailors when O'Hara arrived with the news that he had arranged for Li Yen, a local merchant, to take delivery of the pearl-shell cargo. By midday the shell was unloaded and paid for, stores, fuel and water were aboard, and O'Hara appeared with his gear to join the ship. Dirk completed the usual ship's business at the customs house and, as soon as he was back aboard, they let go the mooring ropes and got the ship under way.

With her auxiliary motor throbbing, the white schooner cleared the harbour and slid slowly out to sea until she began to swing and plunge in the blue Gulf rollers. Then the motor was cut, all sail was set and the *Jolo* lay over under a press of canvas, outward bound on the trail of Alimud Din and the secret of Cordovada Island.

Chapter Eight

A Kunjang Story

In squally monsoon weather the *Jolo* made the trip over the Western Pacific to Kunjang in four days, and one clear, warm but rather wild morning the schooner raised the island dead ahead of her plunging bowsprit.

Kunjang was a low wooded island with little to offer sightseers. There was a tiny natural harbour with a breakwater and a jetty, a few cargo sheds, a general store, and a radio station manned by American Navy personnel under the command of a Lieutenant Mason, who acted as a liaison officer between the headman of Tano village and the USA administration centre at Palau.

The island population consisted of a few hundred Kanakas, some Chamorros – people of mixed Kanaka and Spanish ancestry – and less than a dozen whites. These included the radio-station crew, two or three planters, a schoolteacher and an old retired German missionary. The health of the community was supervised by a Government vessel, which acted as a floating clinic, visiting all the local islands at fixed intervals.

Dirk navigated the *Jolo* through the outer reef passages into a shallow lagoon and eventually brought his craft alongside the jetty. When they arrived the harbour was sheltering a naval launch, a mission boat, a battered island schooner, and a number of fishing boats. Palm-tree flats and mangrove swamps bordered the shore hereabouts.

A youthful naval rating had come down to meet the schooner, to present Lieutenant Mason's compliments and invite the *Jolo*'s skipper to call on him. The weather was clearing, though the wind was still high, when Dirk and Jim walked up to the administrative office which was adjacent to the radio station. And Lieutenant Mason, a tall, brisk, purposeful officer, was waiting to greet them.

'It's an event to see a new face around here,' he told them as he led the way into his office where he invited them to take a seat and join him in having some coffee.

'Has any other vessel called here in the last few days?' Dirk inquired.

'Just the usual monthly trading schooner from Koror,' Mason said. 'If we didn't have radio contact here we might as well be on the moon.' He quickly examined Dirk's papers and asked some routine questions about the ship's business. Dirk explained that he wanted permission to prospect pearling grounds in the vicinity of Kunjang.

'We would like to encourage a pearling industry around here so I'll do all I can to help,' Mason promised. 'I can let you have a provisional permit right away and you can get straight on with your prospecting. In the meantime I'll contact my Koror headquarters, just in case there are any snags. Frankly I don't think you will find business very profitable in this territory.'

'Don't you have any local pearling outfits?' Jim asked.

'There used to be an industry here before the Second World War,' Mason answered, 'but the lagoon got worked out and the Kanakas don't take kindly to working with apparatus in the deep waters outside the reefs. We have a family of Chamorros who used to go pearling and diving. Now they rely on fishing to make a living. Two brothers of them worked as divers for the Japanese firm that tried to refloat the wreck on Cordovada reef three years ago.'

'Did you say a wreck on Cordovada reef?' Jim queried.

Mason grinned broadly. 'Oh, man, don't start hoping for salvage money! The wreck is a Japanese freighter that got her navigation mixed up one dirty night three years back. The crew were all saved but the ship went hard aground. A month later a Jap salvage firm had a notion of cutting the ship in two, blowing the reef with dynamite and refloating the stern half, but the idea misfired. I'm told the Chamorro brothers worked on the job, but when a Jap diver was lost they quit, and the salvage firm gave up.'

'How was the diver lost?' Dirk asked.

'I don't know,' Mason said frankly. 'It was before I came out y'know. I think the poor man got trapped on the bottom while he was planting dynamite charges. Some of us have been out there with the navy launch and it's a nasty place, all reefs and tide-rips.'

'Cordovada will be the island that lies due south of here,' Dirk suggested.

'Nine miles due south. It's just a great rock overgrown with jungle in parts, all caves and holes, with a loop of reefs attached. I believe it's a part of the rim of a sunken volcano crater.'

'We had an idea to try our luck out there,' Dirk explained. 'We've an Irishman in our crew who was here years ago. He says there's a yarn about Cordovada Island being haunted that keeps the Kunjang people away.'

Mason chuckled at this statement. 'Come to think of it, your Irishman's right! But all these islands have their local ghosts. They say a mad Spaniard haunts Cordovada Island, and if anybody sets eyes on the spectre he won't live another day! The Kanakas certainly believe the story, but it doesn't bother the Chamorros. They go out there to fish regularly and sometimes use the wreck for a night or two's lodgings.'

'Who was the mad Spaniard? Does anybody know his history?'

'No good asking me,' Mason said brusquely, 'but if you're interested you should talk to Herr Reidel, the retired German missionary who lives on the hill. He's Kunjang's oldest inhabitant – must be ninety years old if he's a day. He came out here more than fifty years ago. He knows all the folk-tales and history there is to know, and I understand he salvaged a lot of manuscripts and records from the ruins of a church which was built by Spanish Jesuits more than a hundred and fifty years ago.'

'Herr Reidel sounds very interesting,' Dirk remarked. 'We'd very much like to have a talk with him if it can be arranged.'

'Nothing easier,' Mason said. 'Herr Reidel lives about half a mile up the hill road from the harbour, and he never leaves his house nowadays. I'll send a messenger to advise him you would like to call.'

'That's very good of you. What would be a convenient time for us to see him?'

'Oh, say around seven o'clock this evening. But don't stay too long. The old man tires quickly, you know.'

After this conversation turned into other channels, and soon it was time to go. As Dirk and Jim were walking back along the jetty the pearler skipper came to a halt and pointed over the wind-ruffled blue of the lagoon, across the whitened outer reefs to a violet-hued outline on the southern horizon.

'That must be Cordovada Island,' he said.

Gomez and O'Hara were waiting in the *Jolo*'s saloon cabin which was dense with the smoke of the Irishman's pipe.

'Why, I heard tell o' that Herr Reidel feller when I was out here ten years ago,' O'Hara recollected when he heard what Lieutenant Mason had told them. 'I never did see him but he was reckoned to be a proper old-timer then. I thought he'd be dead long ago. Maybe it would be a shrewd notion to have a chat wid the old man.'

'That's what we mean to do,' Dirk promised him.

'And did you have no news of Alimud Din?' Gomez demanded.

'Not a word. No stranger has landed here in weeks. If Alimud Din is ahead of us he must have gone direct to Cordovada Island.'

'How do you suppose he could have done that if no vessel ever calls there?' the overseer asked.

'Alimud Din is a desperate, determined character,' Dirk said grimly. 'He must have left the liner at Koror three days ago. If he could beg, borrow, steal or even buy a boat at Koror he would make the trip single-handed to Cordovada. In any event he wouldn't want to advertise his business by calling to see Lieutenant Mason.'

They spent the remainder of that day putting the schooner into shape and taking aboard fresh water and stores. Nightfall brought a dead calm and a clear starlit sky. Just after six-thirty a Kanaka arrived with word that Lieutenant Mason had arranged a meeting for them with Herr Reidel at seven o'clock. Dirk had already decided that only he and Jim should visit the old missionary, for obviously a man of such an age would not wish to entertain a large company, especially if it included such a raffish pair as O'Hara and Gomez.

Straightaway he and Jim set off up the hill road from the harbour. It was a bright, smooth, tropical night. Stars were brilliant and a beaming moon was rising behind the island. There was no chance of their missing the way because the solitary road went right past Herr Reidel's door. After a short walk they reached the house, an ancient, stone Spanish-built dwelling with a walled garden and a wooden porch reached by a few stairs.

They were greeted by an elderly Chamorro who led them indoors into a well-lighted room. It was an unexpected apartment to find on a South Sea Island, for the furniture was all old-fashioned European stuff, consisting of cabinets, bookcases, a sideboard, a desk, a Victorian-style suite and even a grand piano.

Herr Reidel awaited them seated in an easy chair and smoking a long-stemmed pipe, a calm patriarchal figure, dressed in a spotlessly white suit which looked too big for his shrunken figure. He had a wise, wrinkled, sun-tanned face and surprisingly alert blue eyes.

He greeted them in a weak guttural voice. 'Forgive me for not getting up, gentlemen, but I am always tired these days. Please be seated. You are very welcome and I hope I can be of assistance to you.'

Dirk and Jim introduced themselves and found seats on a settee with their backs to the window which overlooked the moonlit lagoon.

'Lieutenant Mason kindly sent word that you were coming,' Herr Reidel said. 'I understand that you are interested in the history of Cordovada Island,' he added with a little chuckle.

'That is so, Herr Reidel,' Dirk admitted. 'We're interested in the legend of Cordovada. One of our crew heard this legend when he was out here years ago. We plan to visit the island, and we would like to know its history.'

'What did this member of your crew tell you?' Herr Reidel inquired.

'He told us what the Kunjang natives believe – that the island was named after a Spanish captain, called Cordovada; that his ship was wrecked there centuries ago, and that he and a few survivors reached the shore. They were attacked by head-hunters and they were killed or died, one after another, until Cordovada was left alone. By then the Kunjang people had come to fear the captain and they left him in peace. It was never known how or when he died, but a legend persists that Cordovada still haunts the island and that whoever sees his spectre will shortly die.'

'It is perfectly true, there is such a legend,' the missionary said, watching his visitors keenly. 'But I'm told that you are diving men. Surely you are interested in something besides an old native tale! Tell me the truth now, is it not Spanish treasure that brought you here?'

'That's putting it to us point-blank so we may as well admit we are interested in treasure,' Dirk answered straightforwardly, 'and we suspect it's connected with this Cordovada legend.'

'There is no harm in seeking treasure, my son,' Herr Reidel said with an amiable gesture. 'I have sought that same treasure myself!'

'You mean you've searched Cordovada Island?' Jim exclaimed.

'Of course I have, but I never really expected to find anything, because I do not believe the treasure was ever on the island,' Herr Reidel replied. 'But there was a treasure, and there are records to prove it,' he added, raising a finger significantly.

'Are the Jesuit records still in your possession?' Dirk asked.

The old man shook his head. 'I sent those manuscripts to a Californian museum many years ago, but I still have a record here,' he said, touching his forehead lightly. 'Tell me first why you think there is treasure on Cordovada Island. Surely you have had no access to old Spanish records.'

'We think a treasure exists because the legend of Cordovada is linked with a tradition of the Minganoro tribe of Moros in Mindanao,' Dirk explained. And quite frankly he began to tell Herr

Reidel the principal incidents which had led himself and his ship-mates to Kunjang.

The old missionary listened intently and, despite his age, he was obviously intrigued by Dirk's story. 'That's a thrilling tale!' he said softly when Dirk had finished. 'There was indeed such a man called Don Carlos Legaspi. He was the Conde de Cordovada's son-in-law and he sailed with him from Acapulco on that fateful voyage. So much was established and written in the Jesuit manuscripts – but of course it was never known to the Spaniards that Legaspi had escaped from Cordovada Island and had reached Mindanao. It was supposed he had died with the rest.'

'What is known about the Conde de Cordovada's voyage?' Jim asked restlessly.

'I will tell you what is known,' Herr Reidel answered. 'The Conde de Cordovada was the commander of the *San Nicolas*, one of the annual treasure ships which made the round trip from Acapulco, in Mexico, to Manila in the Philippines. It was in fact the Manila Galleon of 1734.'

'The Manila Galleon,' Dirk repeated softly and wonderingly, for he knew the history of these famous ships which for three centuries had plied their lonely courses across the Pacific Ocean.

Herr Reidel continued quietly with his story. 'In that year of 1734 the *San Nicolas* set sail from Acapulco. The ship carried a large crew, many passengers, and also a complement of soldiers and officials going out to relieve the garrisons of Manila. Besides her other cargo the vessel was carrying the Real Situado – Government bullion, six chests of gold pieces, intended for the Manila Treasury to pay for army, navy and administrative services. At present-day values a million dollars would be a conservative estimate of its worth!'

'That's a fortune indeed,' Jim whispered.

'The *San Nicolas* safely reached the Spanish base on Guam,' Herr Reidel went on. 'Then, after revictualling and refitting, she sailed on the last leg of her trip to make her landfall off Cape Santa Espiritu and thence to Manila. The ship never reached her destination of course. Within two days she was dismasted in a typhoon.

Completely disabled, she drifted southwards in high seas until a second storm threw her upon Cordovada Island.

'The Spanish records state that the Kunjang people estimated that a score of survivors were alive on the island, but these quickly dwindled from hardships and native attacks. After that the records merely confirm the tale that has given rise to the legend of Cordovada.'

'Then there is no written record of treasure ever being salvaged?' Dirk queried.

'If the Real Situado had ever been recovered there must have been some record,' the missionary said. 'Jesuit missionaries were established on Kunjang less than forty years after the disaster and they believed the treasure had sunk irretrievably with the galleon.'

'But they couldn't have known about Legaspi's escape to Mindanao,' Jim put in.

'They had no knowledge of Legaspi's venture,' Herr Reidel stated. 'Doubtless Legaspi made the voyage with two or three picked men on Conde de Cordovada's orders, possibly in a native canoe or one of the galleon's boats. But he did not succeed in reaching Manila, so the records have no mention of him other than to list him as one of the *San Nicolas*'s company. And there is another vital fact which was unknown to the Jesuit historians,' Reidel added with a touch of sly mystery in his manner. 'They did not know the actual place where the *San Nicolas* foundered!'

'Is there some trace of the galleon?' Dirk asked quickly.

Herr Reidel's aged but lively eyes considered the pearler skipper with a touch of triumph. 'On Kunjang we have a Chamorro family, Marlo Vajas and his two sons, Luis and Leon, who go fishing around Cordovada Island and sometimes even shelter for a night or two aboard the Japanese wreck which lies out there on the reef.'

'Lieutenant Mason mentioned them,' Dirk said.

'They used to be pearl-divers,' Herr Reidel went on. 'The father of them, whom I know well, once told me an intriguing tale. He was diving for pearl-oyster, using an old patched-up helmet dress, in Cordovada lagoon. It is a deep lagoon, actually the basin of a submerged volcano crater. There was an accident and by some negligence the Chamorro's lines were left untended, and before he could be held he had slipped down an underwater slope into the middle of the lagoon. Before he was hauled up he recovered consciousness on the lagoon floor. He was very deep – over thirty fathoms, he says – and he recalls the vision of a great *coral wreck*.'

'A coral wreck!' Jim repeated incredulously.

'The Chamorro has always persisted in his story, but it is only fair to say that his brain is affected,' Herr Reidel said solemnly. 'He suffered a severe attack of compressed-air illness which not only crippled his body but his mind too, and he never dived again. Everyone else, even his own sons, believes that the coral wreck is a fantasy of his disordered mind.'

'But you believe the coral wreck is the remains of the *San Nicolas*,' Dirk stated frankly.

'It is a logical belief,' Herr Reidel said sagely. 'In heavy weather a wooden vessel like the galleon could easily have been carried over the reefs into the lagoon. I am convinced the *San Nicolas* and its treasure lie very close to Cordovada Island, and all the more so since I have heard your part of the tale. I think Alonso de Cordovada sent Legaspi off with a secret message concerning the location of the treasure in the hilt of his own sword. He remained on that barren place all those years hoping his henchman would return with assistance to salvage the Real Situado, for as commander of the Manila Galleon he would not dare or even wish to return home without it!'

'If the galleon foundered in such deep water – thirty fathoms or more – Cordovada could never have hoped to salvage the treasure,' Dirk pointed out.

'That's a problem, but the ship might not have been lying so deep in those days. This whole area is volcanic. Upheavals and subsidence are constantly taking place. It occurs to me that the floor of the Cordovada lagoon might have been steadily sinking for two centuries.'

Herr Reidel chuckled and shrugged his thin shoulders doubtfully.

'Of course these ideas are all theory and wishful thinking, but there is little I can do myself these days except sit and dream. The proof of the matter can only be established by men with diving equipment like yourselves.'

'You say the coral wreck lies somewhere in the middle of the lagoon,' Dirk said. 'It might be a difficult job to locate it in such deep water.'

'The lagoon is split by a high, rock bluff,' Reidel told them. 'The Japanese wreck lies on the reef north of the bluff. The coral wreck, according to the Chamorro, is in the deepest part of the lagoon, two hundred yards due south of the extremity of the bluff.'

'We will go out there and take a look,' Dirk said.

And now Herr Reidel reached for an ivory-topped stick beside his chair and with the aid of it he got slowly and stiffly to his feet. 'I have told you everything I know, and I wish you good fortune,' he said sincerely. 'If you dive in the Cordovada lagoon come back and tell me about it. Before I die I would like to know if the coral wreck is fact or fable.'

The two pearlers shook hands with the old missionary, said good-bye and left his house. When they got back to the *Jolo* they found Gomez and O'Hara eager for news, and Dirk wasted no time in relating everything the missionary had said.

'So the treasure exists! The Real Situado is as good as under our hatches already!' Gomez cried delightedly when Dirk had finished. 'We shall all of us live in luxury for the rest of our lives.'

'Ye're forgettin' another party has designs on that treasure and probably has better information about it than we do ourselves,' O'Hara warned. 'That thievin' Moro must have reached Koror and from there I'm sure he'd swim the whole distance to Cordovada wid a knife between his teeth for six chests o' gold!'

'If that gold lies thirty fathoms deep Alimud Din will have no better chance of getting it than he did the Sword of Cordovada,' Dirk said reassuringly. 'Let's all turn in and tomorrow we'll see what Cordovada Island looks like.'

Chapter Nine

Mystery Island

Early next morning the *Jolo* slipped her moorings and worked her
way out to sea under motor power. Beyond the reefs sail was set
and, close-hauled on a stiff wind, she stood to the south for Cordovada Island.

The island was in sight all the way, and before the sun was well
up the schooner was close to her objective – a rugged basalt rock,
recovered in places with green jungle growth, situated on the
eastern edge of a surf-ringed loop of reefs and islets. The formation
was the rim of a submerged volcano crater, as Herr Reidel had told
them, and the island itself was the only part of the formation where
natural rock protruded above sea-level. The reefs and islets were
merely coral growth rising from the sunken volcano rim.

The *Jolo*'s crew dowsed their fore and mainsails and hove to half
a mile north of the reef under a single staysail. The sunshine was
bright, but still it remained a doubtful restless sort of day. A lot of
cumulus cloud showed white as snow around the horizon and the
damp, moody monsoon wind whipped white crests on the fast blue
swells.

With his three companions Dirk stood amidships on the rolling,
creaking, spray-wet schooner, studying the lonely scene. Cordovada Island, on the eastern edge of the reef ring, was a rock some
fifty acres in area, precipitous on its seaward side but sloping down
to sandy coves on the inner lagoon beach, except in one spot where
a lofty jungle-crowned bluff extended half-way into the lagoon.

'Yonder's the Jap wreck!' O'Hara boomed above the rumble of surf and wind. He pointed a brown powerful arm across the port bow to where the reef adjoined the northern side of the island.

Dirk trained his binoculars on the wreck. It had been a large freighter, and it lay with its bows across the reef flat, its stern awash in the surf.

'It's a grim-lookin' solitude it is, to be sure,' O'Hara declared. He stood towering over his shipmates, dressed in rolled-up breeches, sandals and a blue faded shirt fluttering in the wind, his peaked cap pulled hard down over his scowling black brows. 'God damn me eyes, if I was a poor ghost I'd never haunt such a lonely place, for it would scare the livin' daylights out o' me it would.'

'I don't see a boat of any sort,' Dirk said as he methodically scanned the coves and beaches within view. 'If Alimud Din got here he must have had a boat.'

'A small-size boat could be easily concealed,' Jim pointed out.

'I guess you're right, Jim. He wouldn't leave a boat in plain view. We'll anchor in the lagoon, then go ashore and search the island.'

Soon the *Jolo* was under way again, this time with her engine throbbing, and she rolled considerably under bare poles. Gomez was sent aloft to watch for submerged rocks or coral heads, and Dirk conned the ship with extreme caution for he had no chart of this locality. He took his vessel wide of the fringing reef then brought her about from the west, heading for a passage between two flat islets. Here the tide ran blue and deep, raising a chattering crush of foam at the ship's stem.

Suddenly there came a hail from the foremast top where Gomez, taut and vigilant, was watching the coral fangs lining the reef passage. 'Señor Rogers! A boat aground – on the reef – to port!'

Dirk, at the ship's wheel, threw a glance in the direction of Gomez's thrusting arm. O'Hara and Jim moved instantly to the port rails. They all saw the wreckage of an upturned boat lodged irretrievably in a coral gully on the little islet less than fifteen yards away on their port beam. It looked like a sailing cutter some twenty-five feet in length, and it was a hopeless wreck.

There was no time to comment as the *Jolo* swept through the reef passage into the lagoon. White coral glimmered under the schooner's keel, then the lagoon bottom fell away quickly into unknown depths and the vessel glided smoothly on calm waters. Dirk kept his ship under way until she came under the lee of the south cliff of the bluff. Here an anchor was let go and the schooner was brought up gently.

'What do'you think about that boat wreck on the edge of the reef passage?' Jim asked his skipper.

'It looked like a sailing cutter. It certainly wasn't a native craft from around these parts. I'd say it was wrecked very recently because it will soon be knocked to matchwood in that surf.'

'We never heard of any boat being missing from Kunjang,' Jim said. 'It's the sort of craft Alimud Din could have stolen at Koror. He could have made the trip in a boat like that single-handed.'

'If he did, it looks as though he has saved us all a heap o' trouble and got himself drowned,' O'Hara growled.

'If the Moro got as close to Cordovada Island as the reef passage he would not drown. His lust for gold would keep him afloat!' Gomez exclaimed vehemently.

'There has been some nasty weather in the last few days,' Dirk remarked thoughtfully. 'If Alimud Din made the trip from Koror he could easily have got piled on the reef as he tried to enter the lagoon, because that boat had no engine.'

Now they were able to study Cordovada Island at close quarters in the lee of the bluff, an eighty-foot-high rampart which, from their anchorage, concealed from view the northern side of the lagoon and the Japanese wreck.

O'Hara in particular was deeply impressed by the solitude, wildness and no doubt the history of the island. For here was no sign of human presence, just the timeless rocks and reefs cradled in the blue ocean and lulled by the perpetual thunder of surf, the moan of the wind and the eerie shrieking of sea-birds which winged above the schooner's mast-heads.

'Ah, there might be anythin' at all up there,' the Irishman declared huskily as he scowled at the rugged bluff, then uneasily shifted his gaze towards the interior of the island. 'There might be anythin' at all watchin' and waitin' y'know. Alimud Din must have a brave black heart in him if he can bring himself to prowl around such a place on his lonesome.'

Dirk did not waste time in conjectures about Alimud Din's character. He had decided to search the island and he gave orders to launch the ship's dinghy. Soon they were all aboard the small boat and had pushed off from the schooner. In the lee of the bluff the lagoon was like a mill-pond. They beached the dingy and Dirk led the way ashore. Red robber crabs scuttled aside from their path; and some of these tough crustaceans could be seen high in the coconut palms where they'd climbed to cut down the fruit.

Dirk advanced from the beach into a gully alongside the bluff. Here a thin stream of water drained into the lagoon, and he followed this winding waterway inshore with his companions following silently and vigilantly. Very soon the gully opened abruptly into a basin-shaped hollow where a shallow pool was fed by a modest waterfall gushing over a rock ledge at the farther side of the hollow. Except for the rushing music of the waterfall it was immensely quiet here, as though time were standing still. Clumps of ferns and palms grew amidst the rocks on the surrounding slopes and the edges of the pool were colourful with flowering shrubs and tropical blossoms.

'There are many places a man might lie hid on this small island,' Gomez observed as he gazed suspiciously around the peaceful scene.

'Our best plan will be to fan out from this place and work our way right around the island perimeter,' Dirk directed.

For two hours they searched, first examining all the dips and hollows in the island interior then gradually working outwards to tour the cliff-tops on the seaward side and the beaches and bluff facing into the lagoon. With the enigma of the recently-wrecked cutter fresh in their minds they searched warily, but they saw nothing of the Moro, or of any stranger, or any sign of men ever being there.

They completed their search on the north side of the bluff and from there the wreck of the Japanese freighter was in plain view, looming like some stricken leviathan across the reef. Cloud shadows were spreading a gloom over the sea-scape, but at intervals bursts of sunshine, brilliant and dazzling, would turn the reefs as white as porcelain and illuminate the battered rusted hull of the wreck.

'There's a pilot ladder made fast amidships on that wreck,' Dirk pointed out. 'I wonder how long it has been there.'

'It's three years since salvage men worked aboard. The Chamorro fishermen might use the ladder. They spend nights aboard, so we've been told,' Jim observed.

That lonely rope-ladder dangling down the bulging hull of the wreck was like a question-mark, so Dirk decided to investigate the Japanese ship. They went back to the beach where they'd left the dinghy, then instead of returning to the schooner they rowed around the bluff and across the north side of the lagoon. The wind was rising and there was a moan on the sea when they made their boat fast and climbed on to the dangerous honeycomb of the reef flat.

Now the wreck loomed over them like a crumbling iron castle, its bow lifted so high a man could walk beneath it, its stern awash in deep water. The hull was alive with eerie booms, thuds and creaks caused by wind and tide, and sounding as though a giant poltergeist had made its home within.

'Sure and it's a pitiful thing a wreck is,' O'Hara said as he dubiously scanned the barnacle-encrusted hull where it lay with its bottom plates skewered by the coral fangs. 'It's a wonder the entire vessel hasn't slipped over the reef edge in all these years. I wouldn't wonder if it wasn't a thousand fathoms deep just one long hop, skip and a jump to seaward.'

Dirk tackled the pilot ladder first and he soon climbed over the ship's rail amidships. It was obvious that salvage men had been at work in an effort to cut the after part of the ship clean away from the foredeck and bows. There were gaping holes where plates had been removed and a great split across the midship deck. Dirk was joined by his shipmates and together they looked briefly around the upper works. They made a discovery in the ship's galley, for it was evident that some cooking had been done there not long ago, and they assumed the Chamorro fishermen must have been aboard quite recently.

They found nothing else of interest in the bare gutted deck-houses, so they descended a companion-way into the gloom of the main saloon cabin. This place had apparently been used by salvage men as a store-room for they had gone leaving some crates and a jumble of gear and tackle. There was even a battered diver's helmet with the faceglass shattered, possibly a memento of disaster conveniently left behind. It was Gomez, poking under a heap of burlap, who made a startling find.

'Señor Rogers, look here!' he cried excitedly. And when Dirk joined him the overseer pointed at a stout box fitted with padlocks and a hinged lid. But it was unlocked and Gomez had turned back the lid. The box was half full of neatly-packed cartridges of gelatine dynamite.

'That's a dangerous cargo to leave behind,' Jim remarked grimly.

'Maybe the salvage crew left in a big hurry,' Gomez suggested with an uncomfortable grin as he replaced the tight-fitting lid.

'Listen!' Dirk broke in softly. He held up a warning hand. Jim and Gomez looked at him uncertainly. Then they heard footsteps distantly above their heads on deck. Dirk peered around the gloomy saloon, and suddenly he laughed reassuringly. 'It must be O'Hara. I didn't notice him go up top.'

He'd scarcely spoken when they heard a loud hail from the deck. It was O'Hara calling them. They hurried up the companion-way and out on to the windswept deck. O'Hara was standing by the midship starboard rails, his shirt and breeches fluttering in the breeze, and he was pointing across the lagoon. He made a wild dark figure as he turned a haggard gaze on them, still with his arm outstretched.

'There he goes! I seen him wid me own eyes!'

'What have you seen, man?' Dirk demanded as he reached the ship's rails.

'*The spectre of Cordovada!*'

They all gripped the rusted rails on the listing deck. The tide was creeping over the reef and soon they would need to wade if they wanted to reach their dingy. The wind was rising and the sky was overcast, but a weird silvery glow illuminated the lagoon. Following O'Hara's pointing arm they were in time to see a grey waterspout, looking like a giant scarecrow, travel eerily across the lagoon and vanish beyond the bluff.

'That's no spectre, it's a waterspout!'

O'Hara was panting. His chest heaved powerfully and sweat stood in droplets on his strong, dark face. He shook his head and looked bemusedly from one to the other.

'I seen the spectre,' he said hollowly.

A stronger gust of wind brought stinging rain with it and the surf boomed awesomely over the half-submerged poop deck of the wreck.

'It is an evil omen,' Gomez said huskily as though the words were forced out of him.

'There's a squall coming, perhaps worse,' Dirk said practically. 'We had better get back aboard the schooner and snug her down for the night. Tomorrow I will make a dive into the lagoon and find out if the old Chamorro was speaking the truth about the coral wreck.'

Chapter Ten

The Coral Wreck

There was quite a blow that night. The wind reached gale force and the ocean groaned and strained about Cordovada Island like a Titan trying to wrench it from its foundations. Even in the reef-embayed lagoon the *Jolo* rode roughly at her moorings, and her crew spent a restless night, disturbed by the shock and thunder of surf jamming in coral caverns and wailing through organ-like blowholes in the reef.

Dirk had taken the precaution of setting an anchor watch and each man of the crew took his turn to pace the wild rain-swept deck throughout the night.

In the black early morning hours, however, the storm passed its peak and after that began to die quickly. By dawn the wind had dropped to nothing, and first light came with serene beauty as the island scene emerged from the dark hours like a painting taking form and colour under a master's brush. The lagoon was like glass and the palms on the reef islets seemed modelled in wax. Beyond the sheltering reefs the ocean still growled moodily, but it was blue and breath-taking to the farthest horizons. There was no doubt that Dirk had a perfect day to make his dive.

After an early breakfast the schooner's crew hove up anchor and moved their vessel into a position two hundred yards due south of the bluff extremity where, if Herr Reidel was right, the old Chamorro pearler had made his last dive. Dirk supervised the mooring of the schooner for a deep dive, with two bow anchors laid out ahead and a kedge anchor astern. Then Jim took a sound and found bottom at thirty-six fathoms.

'Two hundred and sixteen feet! This is a mighty deep lagoon and no mistake,' the schooner mate commented with a hard look at his shipmates.

'It is deeper than a church steeple is high,' Gomez declared huskily, and he gazed round-eyed and dismayed over the schooner's rail into the misty blue beneath the hull.

'The Chamorro was near the mark about the depth,' Dirk said. 'I'll get my gear on and go down right away. Double 'seventies' should serve me, Jim, and I'll use a distance line from a shotrope.'

They got busy with their preparations at once and the necessary gear was brought on deck. A midship bulwark section was removed on the port side and a shotrope, weighted with a cement-filled oil drum, was run down from the schooner's deck. Then O'Hara and Gomez were set to work rigging out a diving ladder which was clamped to a frame to keep it clear of the ship's hull.

After that Dirk began to get into his diving rig. Despite the temperature on deck – it was just nine o'clock and rising eighty degrees in the middle of the lagoon – the pearler skipper decided to wear a heavy-duty neoprene suit with hood attached, for two hundred feet deep he knew the sea must be icy cold, and as he got into this outfit Jim began charging up the twin, plastic-covered, yellow tanks, each with seventy cubic feet of air.

Soon the hard drumming of the air-compressor was throwing sharp echoes back from the slopes of the island bluff which jutted into the lagoon like a castle bastion. The *Jolo*'s compressor was a three-stage unit, capable of attaining the high air pressures required for the tanks of self-contained equipment. It was also used to serve a continuous surface supply, via an attached reservoir, for other types of diving gear.

At last, masked and fin-footed, with his tanks hooked up, Dirk was ready to go, and he made a somewhat sinister-looking figure really, as though within the space of a few minutes he had been transformed into an alien being from another planet.

'Give me a rifle-shot warning after twelve minutes, Jim,' he told his partner, then he moved to the diving ladder, and for a few moments scanned the view to seaward.

Way out beyond the surf-tumbled fringing reef the ocean had grown calm, just heaving with an oily blue swell, and the young skipper caught sight of the pale iridescent crest of a physalia jellyfish, called a Portuguese Man o' War, half drifting and half sailing across the wind, after its peculiar fashion, a deceptively innocent-looking but dangerous animal, for it carried a sting powerful enough to incapacitate a swimmer.

And inside the reefs, within the lagoon, a hefty eagle ray took his eye as it breached off the schooner's port bow, and he watched the blanket shape twisting like an aircraft in a mortal spin till it thudded back on the water in a shower of spray. Perhaps the ray was trying to stun smaller fish, ridding itself of parasites, or maybe a shark was after it.

Dirk did not make a crash entry. Diving was too much of a job of work for him, and he knew he might have a long arduous day ahead. As a working diver he always conserved his energy for an emergency when it might be needed desperately. Besides, by nature he was a deliberate type, who could move quickly if necessary, but who never made a habit of rushing. So he turned to face inboard and methodically started down the diving ladder. In doing so he glanced ahead, past the ship's bows, and he was just in time to see a heavy swirl or 'slick' where a large creature had passed close to the surface right under the *Jolo*'s bowsprit.

The incident evidently gave him food for thought, for after a moment's consideration he looked up at Jim, who was watching him. 'I reckon I'd better take the gas gun down with me,' he told his partner with the glimmer of a grin. 'That weapon gives me a lot of moral support!'

As Dirk waited for the gun he slipped the ties on a big iron shackle, placed there by Jim, and which he meant to use as an additional sinker to take him to the bottom. In another moment he was handed the underwater gun, a weapon with pistol-grip and twin triggers that fired steel darts powered by carbon dioxide cartridges, and which for the time being he slung over his shoulder.

Then he inserted his mouthpiece and started breathing from his tanks, and another two steps down the ladder took him right under the surface where he was suddenly festooned by a burst of his exhaust air bubbles.

Unlike the old helmet-type diver, whose air pressure inside his helmet was stepped up by the pump to meet the rising water pressure as he descended, Dirk's self-contained gear allowed him to carry air at over two thousand five hundred pounds per square inch in his tanks, fed to him by the ingenuity of his regulator and valves at a pressure always just above that of the surrounding water whatever his depth.

Aboard the *Jolo* they had a variety of diving gear, including rigid helmet outfits, which were usually more comfortable for commercial jobs, where a diver had to stay down for excessively long periods in one spot, using a cutting torch or doing repair work. But for a reconnaissance dive Dirk always preferred to use the free-ranging self-contained swimfin gear which required far less manipulation and was proof against most of the fearsome 'pressure' dangers inherent in the rigid helmet dress, such as being blown spreadeagled to the surface by a jammed exhaust valve, or what was worse, suffering a sudden 'fall' when the sea weight rose faster than the surface pump could cope with it and a terrible water squeeze ensued. But other dangers still remained with the new equipment – the bends, oxygen poisoning, nitrogen narcosis, air embolisms and of course with self-contained gear the additional hazard of running out of air!

The lagoon was crystal clear this morning and calm as a woodland lake. As he stood there on the bottom rung of the diving ladder Dirk could see the hull of his schooner curving smoothly through the shining water into the sternpost. There were lots of fish, apparently attracted by the shelter of the schooner – dashing battalions of tiny silversides, several large topes, a species of shark, twisting like eels beneath the rudder and, where the starboard anchor chain slanted down, he saw a school of red snappers, ugly foot-long spinous-finned fish, moving lethargically like a thundercloud.

Hampered somewhat by his shackle sinker and the underwater

gun over his shoulder, Dirk looked around for the shotrope, and he found it within arm's reach by his right side. He gripped the rope, wrapped his legs about it, and began his long slide into the blue gulf under the *Jolo*'s gently-swaying hull.

He went down as rapidly as he felt was consistent with safety, for though his large double-tank capacity would last him nearly two hours close to the surface, at two hundred feet deep, where he needed his air at around ninety pounds per square inch, he would use it fast. This was why he had warned Jim to let him have a gunshot as a signal to ascend if by some mischance he misjudged the duration of his dive.

Once he glanced up, catching a last view of the *Jolo*'s red-painted hull breaking the glittering silver screen of the surface. All around him now the surface blue had changed to a glowing green, but when he looked down it was like gazing over the edge of a skyscraper in a summer dusk, with no mark to serve as a guide to distance.

At about fifty feet deep Dirk experienced a dull powerful sensation of pressure over his eyes, and his ears ached. He was descending too quickly, so he gripped the shotrope and checked his fall. There was now a perceptible current, pressing on him like a breeze, and the sea was much cooler. There were still plenty of fish; this tropical lagoon was a prolific breeding-ground; and he saw packs of striped mullet, gay sea perch, predaceous houndfish and halfbeaks and colourful wrasse and, as he rested there on the shotrope, he was surprised by a shoal of tiny squids sweeping past his divemask, bulging-eyed miniature monsters, pumping their mantles like tiny jet engines.

Dirk waited just a few moments until his head cleared, then, as he was about to resume his descent, he was aware of a movement in the darker green beneath him, a movement which quickly resolved itself into a great blue-backed shape impressive with sinister grace. It was a very big shark, and in another moment Dirk recognised the animal as a mako or blue pointer, fifteen feet from snout to tail if it was an inch, and half a ton in weight. Viewed under water, and particularly from this acute angle, it seemed a veritable juggernaut.

Despite a considerable acquaintance with these sea tigers Dirk experienced a warning tingle in his nerve-ends as the giant fish spiralled towards him. For the mako ranked next to the killer whale and the white man-eater shark as one of the most dangerous and unpredictable beasts in the ocean. Without shifting his gaze from the shark he was aware that all the fish in the vicinity had vanished, and he wished fervently that he had the same capacity for getting out of sight quickly. However, not being blessed with any cloak of invisibility he stayed where he was on the shotrope, and the thought went through his mind that this must be the creature which had made that large-scale movement on the surface just before he submerged.

The shark rose as it if were on the crest of an invisible fountain blowing it up from the depths, swinging at the same time with idle movements of its powerful tail. The mako – blue pointer, blue porpoise shark or snapper shark, as it was variously known — was an open-water fish, and Dirk surmised that this one had haphazardly entered the lagoon on the flood of last night's storm and now, after a perfunctory exploration, was getting edgy to find a way out again.

It swayed up to divemask level and Dirk had an unenviable view of the monster as it hung suspended on wide-spread downward-pointing pectoral fins, like some futuristic space craft. Then it glided astern of him and he turned on the shotrope to keep it in sight. He was in something of a quandary, for to use his underwater gun he would have to jettison his shackle sinker, and possibly spoil his dive. He dared not hook the sinker to his belt, for if anything happened to him and he lost consciousness it would drag him irretrievably to the bottom. On the other hand, if he waited any longer to use his gun it might be too late.

When he got the mako into view again it was approaching, not swiftly as it must do if it meant to attack, but curiously as a bullock will challenge a dog. Possibly it was simply lured by the intermittent stream of air bubbles that erupted from this alien creature, suspended like a spider on a thread from some other world above the surface.

Dirk saw an icy robot eye set far back from the snout and he glimpsed sabre teeth as the shark swung its head to get him into focus with one eye after the other. When it was twelve feet away Dirk dragged in a breath which he let go forcibly around his mouthpiece in a watery shout. The mako jibbed as though it had been hit on the snout; then it veered with a white flash of its belly and lunged upward and away in a swirl of water that beat against Dirk like a tidal wave.

Almost immediately the young skipper loosed his grip and recommenced his slide to the bottom, fairly confident that the mako would not follow him into really deep water. Now he was inexorably adding fathoms of water above him and he began to feel the pinch of cold on his unprotected hands, as his sinker, weights and gear dragged him steadily into a grey-green quietude, a deep-sea silence where a diver's isolation becomes a tangible thing, dark as a shadow beside him, a silence broken just by the harsh intake of his own breathing and the whistle of his exhaust bubbles, growing shriller and more glassy with the depth.

His depth gauge, glimmering like an eye in a forest gloom, showed just over the thirty-two-fathom mark when Dirk found the lagoon bottom. There was light enough to see some thirty feet or so, but it was an emaciated light, haggard from its struggle from the surface, in which objects stood like shadows in a morning mist.

Dirk was no stranger to deep diving, but all the same he was strongly conscious of the burden of his air pressure, which caused a slowing in his thinking and reflex actions. He let go the iron shackle and watched a delicate sea fan crumble beneath its weight. The cement-filled oil drum, anchoring the shotrope, was ground into the glimmering coral beside him. Startled by his presence a tiny octopus vanished under a huge scallop shell in a cloud of brown sepia; and with bared teeth a green moray eel withdrew its head into a crevice.

Dirk gave a signal on the shotrope to indicate that he had touched bottom. Then he checked his time and his air supply. Already he had used a quarter of one tank. His encounter with the shark had delayed him. The distance or guide line he was carrying was fitted with a small spring shackle, and he slipped this on to the shotrope. Then, underwater gun in hand, he prepared to reconnoitre his surroundings.

A current was flowing, stronger here than on the surface, and it was as cold as charity. And on coming so quickly down from the warm surface waters, even protected by his rubber suit, Dirk felt like a man who has walked out of a Turkish bath into a refrigerator. He shivered as he peered ahead through his divemask.

The bottom where he had landed was all coral, possibly red or yellow in daylight, but down here at this depth, it showed only in blue and grey tones; and spreading sea fans, waving weeds and the furtive movements of fish and crustaceans evoked a weird haunted atmosphere that chilled a man's blood as much as the cold current. Then as Dirk's eyes grew accustomed to the poor light, and his senses got adjusted to the strains of pressure, he began to discern a startling symmetry around him.

He began swimming slowly over an uneven spread of blue coral. A looming shadow ahead emerged into a coral column that lost itself in the sea above. A dark barrier looked like a reef, but when he turned along it he came upon an encrusted balustrade beyond which there was nothing but water, for the sea bottom lay over an edge in deeper gloom.

Once again Dirk explored the barrier, and soon he discovered what was undoubtedly an artificial form – an old-time ship's ladder still recognisable under its coral sheath. Half-frozen by this time, but cheered tremendously by his success, Dirk eventually convinced himself that the barrier was simply the break of an old-fashioned sailing ship's quarter-deck. That balustrade must be a bulwark along the deck edge, and the column he had passed would be the remains of a mast. Without a doubt he had touched bottom on the old Chamorro's coral wreck!

Dirk carried on, rising in the current and paying out his guide line as he went. He passed another mast – the mizzen, for he realised he was swimming aft – and a broken yard or boom, lying encrusted across the quarter-deck. He followed the unmistakable 'tumble-home' of a galleon's hull into a narrow, lofty, high-pooped stern, then he sheered inboard, finding more fossilised deck-fittings and a ship's wheel standing sentinel in the watery silence.

The pearler skipper gripped the wheel – it was as solid and still as if it had grown there – and he rested for a few moments, protected from the mauling current. He was chilled to the marrow, his hands were losing all sense of touch, but his heart beat excitedly. For he was confident this ancient petrified hulk could be none other than the *San Nicolas*, the eighteenth-century Manila Galleon, the last command of the Conde Alonso de Cordovada! And surely somewhere beneath the coral and the timbers must be the captain's stateroom, and somewhere under that the lazaret or strongroom which held the Real Situado – six chests of Spanish gold!

This idea brought with it a sobering reflection, for on his way aft from the shotrope Dirk had seen no gaping hold, or hatchway or companion-way or scuttle or cabin door or passage. All must have been filled and enshrouded by the creeping coral. He wondered if the entire hull were sealed like this, or was there a gap or a crack somewhere about the stern where a diver could gain access to the vital part of the ship?

When he moved on again he felt the tug of his guide line. He had reached the end of it, but he was determined to examine the stern of the galleon, so he made the line fast to the ship's wheel and went on without it. He swam over the taffrail and sank down by the stern. Here were galleries, gun ports and cabin windows festooned and masked by coral, and lastly the remnants of a rudder. Even in the eerie half-light Dirk realised that the galleon really was a coral wreck, cemented by living organisms into the lagoon floor.

The current was even stronger and colder under the stern and he was glad to rise back to the level of the ship's deck. Just above the taffrail he saw a giant black sea bass, a saucer-eyed barrel-mouthed monster fish, some five feet in length and weighing maybe four hundred pounds. It was regarding him venomously, obviously seeing him as an unwelcome intruder to its domain, but there was little danger to be expected from it. Then, as he was untying his guide line from the ship's wheel he heard the crack and shock waves of a rifle shot rippling down through the fathoms. Jim was warning

him about the time. When he looked at his watch Dirk saw that twelve minutes had passed and his air gauge showed he was working on his second tank.

He swam cautiously back to the shotrope with the aid of his guide line, and after giving a signal on the rope he began his ascent. On his way up, back in warmer water, he made several stages, as a precaution against bends, the last and longest at just two fathoms deep, and it was half an hour later when he gripped the diving-ladder rungs and surfaced.

His shipmates were crowding at the head of the ladder to assist him aboard and relieved of mouthpiece and divemask he sank with relief on to a bench amidships. It was good to feel hot sunshine and the fresh breeze on his face, and he grinned into the eager waiting faces about him.

'What did you find, señor?' Gomez demanded, impatient with excitement. 'What did you find down there? Did you find the wreck? Is it there?'

'The wreck is there sure enough. I landed plumb amidships,' Dirk assured them all, 'and believe me, the old Chamorro was right – it's a solid mass of coral!'

'What wreck do you suppose it can be?' Gomez gasped.

'It's the wreck of the *San Nicolas* – the Manila Galleon,' Dirk said confidently.

'How can ye be so sure o' that, man?' O'Hara put in anxiously.

'I'm sure because it's definitely an old galleon, and there's precious little chance of it being any other vessel than the *San Nicolas*.'

'And the treasure – the gold?' Gomez queried, with a look of strained anticipation on his thin, dark features.

'I reckon the treasure must be down there too,' Dirk replied levelly. 'Reidel seems to think so, and he knows more about that galleon and her history than any man living. Most of the old galleons carried treasure and bullion in the lazaret, below the captain's cabin or stateroom. That would be three or four decks down from the quarter-deck.'

'Will you be able to reach this compartment in the wreck?'

Dirk's tanned face looked grimly thoughtful. 'I could reach it easily if any of the hatchways or gun ports were open, but the ship is sealed up with coral, it's as good as solid rock. It lies cold and deep and there's plenty of trouble ahead for anybody who wants to make an entry. Offhand I'd say the best method would be to blast a hole into the main hatch, then go aft along the main deck – blowing whatever bulkheads there are – into the commander's stateroom. From there we could break down into the lazaret, but it could need half a dozen dynamite charges to do it.'

'Dynamite, did ye say?' O'Hara declared, and a sudden exultant grin spread over his unshaven face. 'Man, have ye forgotten? There's a hundredweight o' dynamite in the Jap wreck. Surely it's Fate what made them salvage men leave it there for us.'

'O'Hara is right, of course he is right! There is all the dynamite we need in that iron hulk!' Gomez cried.

'What d'you say to that, Dirk?' Jim demanded, unable to restrain a tremor of excitement at the idea of the great wealth which might lie below.

'If the treasure is there somebody will be going after it, so it may as well be our outfit,' Dirk said soberly. 'Don't imagine we'll do this easily. It might take half a dozen dives, or it might take a hundred!'

'It will be worth it if it takes a hundred days,' O'Hara said.

'I for one cannot wait a hundred days,' Gomez spoke up. 'I cannot wait another moment. Señor Rogers, can we not go at once and collect the dynamite?'

'There's nothing to be gained by waiting,' Dirk agreed. 'You and O'Hara can take the dinghy and pull around the bluff to the Jap wreck. Watch what you're doing with that dynamite. It's dangerous stuff.'

Chapter Eleven

The Chamorros

Perhaps because he had just ascended from the bottom of the lagoon, and the memories of those grey, silent depths were still heavily with him, Dirk was less excited than his shipmates. After all it would be mainly up to him to do the grim and difficult work of salvage, for he was reluctant to allow his partner to share the risks involved. Jim was a good diver, experienced both in pearling and salvage work – but not at thirty-two fathoms deep!

The others, however, were fired with enthusiasm by the golden prospect, and of course the wild and lonely setting for the venture lent a romantic urgency to their quest for the ancient Spanish gold.

So while Jim gave Dirk a hand to attend to his diving gear, Gomez and O'Hara, chuckling and joking to each other, boarded the ship's dinghy and these two, the huge bronzed Irishman and the eager, dark-faced Filipino, made as raffish and piratical a pair as was ever seen afloat. They were soon pulling lustily over the lagoon, singing and shouting so that their voices echoed like spirits calling as they passed under the precipitous cliffs of the bluff which hid the Japanese wreck from view of the schooner's anchorage.

When they had gone and even the sound of their voices had vanished, the pearler skipper and his mate were left sitting on the poop deck of their lazy, sea-worn schooner, feeling as if they were alone in the whole world in an immense quietness, not broken but naturally deepened by the cries of gulls, the solemn roll and boom of reef surf, and the eerie rushes of predatory fish pursuing their prey close by the ship's hull.

'Have you figured how we're going to tackle the job?' Jim asked.

'I've got a few ideas, Jim. Let's go below and think about it over a cup of coffee.'

So they went below decks and while Dirk sat at the saloon-cabin table concentrating with a pencil and a battered notebook Jim brewed some coffee in the galley. Within a few minutes, he rejoined his skipper and placed a cup of coffee at his elbow.

'Wouldn't it be better if we dived together?' Jim suggested.

Dirk shook his head and said positively, 'I want you topside, son, keeping an eye on everything! Gomez and O'Hara have their hearts in the right places but they're short on experience. When I'm searching in that wreck I want somebody on deck I can rely on.'

'How d'you plan to search inside a wreck that's solid coral?'

'I doubt if she's solid, Jim. Coral only grows where there is enough light, so it will all be on the outside of the ship like a layer of cement. I'll be surprised if the *San Nicolas* isn't quite open inside, reasonably so anyhow.'

'But if you think the treasure is in the lazaret why don't you just blow a hole in the stern and get the stuff that way?' Jim asked.

'It will need a big charge to blow her main timbers, Jim, more even than if she were an iron ship. We'd only bring her down in a heap of rubble and have less chance than ever of salvaging the treasure. Besides, we don't have the gear for shifting wreckage at that depth. If I use light charges to blow hatchways, doors and bulkheads, I can keep the whole ship intact until I locate the treasure.

'This is how I estimate the *San Nicolas* would look when she was built,' the pearler skipper went on, pushing his notebook across the table and indicating the sketch he'd made.

Jim studied the rough drawing for a few moments. 'She has as many decks as a cruise liner,' he breathed.

'They built 'em that way in those days, Jim. I reckon the *San*

Nicolas has a quarter-deck, an upper deck, a main gun-deck, a lower gun-deck, then her orlop or store deck, holds and bilges. My plan is to—'

He broke off, and Jim also screwed up his attention, listening keenly. Unquestionably now they could hear the beat of a motor in the lagoon, and they both left the saloon cabin and hurried up on deck. A glance showed them another vessel approaching, about half a cable's length ahead of the *Jolo*'s bows. It was a thirty-foot yawl-rigged fishing boat but the sails were furled and the vessel was under motor power. A noisy cranky engine was thudding in the well abaft a fish-hold.

The boat's crew consisted of two brown-skinned men, one at the helm, the other sitting on the shuddering engine-covers with a lean hand on the gear and throttle controls. Dirk and Jim stayed by the schooner rails watching as this rugged craft came crabwise nearer. They stared hard at the occupants, who both kept grinning cheerfully until they came within speaking distance.

'Can we make fast to your ship, Capitan?' the man at the tiller shouted.

For answer Dirk picked up a heaving line lying on the forehatch top and pitched a few coils across the narrowing gap of sea that separated the two vessels.

'These must be the Chamorro boys we've heard so much about,' Jim said. 'I wonder what they expect to find nosing around here,' he added, eyeing the dubious arrivals very suspiciously.

'Fresh water, grub and anything they can beg, borrow, steal or bulldoze out of us by the looks of them,' Dirk answered.

'Why are you inviting them aboard, then?'

'We're not so busy we can't be hospitable in the middle of the ocean, Jim.'

In another minute the fishing boat bumped against the fenders which Jim had hastily strung by the schooner's hull and the yawl was made fast, bringing with it a pungent whiff of petrol, oil and the odour not only of fresh fish but of very ancient fish impregnated in its timbers.

'Can we come aboard, Capitan?' the man at the tiller cried. 'We are Chamorro men from Kunjang. I am Luis Vajas and this is my little brother Leon.'

'Okay. You can come aboard,' Dirk said.

The barefooted Chamorros came promptly and nimbly over the schooner's bulwarks, both grinning very amiably, with Leon, the younger by a few years, keeping cautiously behind his older and stronger brother.

Luis was wearing just a pair of once-white trousers rolled up to his sinewy calves and a blue peaked cap, apparently donated by one of the American forces on Kunjang. He was an impressive fellow in a sinister sort of way. For while he grinned constantly, showing gleaming unnaturally-large white teeth, his eyes were greedily absorbing information about the schooner and its occupants as a sponge drinks water. His coffee-coloured face was broad, and though the features were regular they were so strong and primitive they appeared ugly. With his dusky chest rippling with muscle, his bowed legs, and grinning expression, he gave the impression of some sort of cheerful sea ape.

Leon, the younger brother, was quite different, apparently having grown up in the shadow of his brother's dominance. He grinned also, but like a simpleton, and his smooth, longish and thin-nosed face had a vacant look with none of the brutish character of Luis's.

'Good-day to you, Capitan, sir, and to you, Mister Mate, sir!' Luis announced in a high-pitched voice, showing wolfish teeth in what was meant to be an engaging smile, and looking very keenly from Dirk to Jim and back again. 'It makes us so happy to meet you. We are just poor fishermen, you understand, so when we see a strange boat in the lagoon we come to pay our respects and perhaps offer our assistance—'

'And find out why you are here, sir!' Leon joined in ingenuously.

At this remark Luis's smiling countenance darkened in a brutal scowl directed at his brother, then turning back to Dirk, with a swift return to kindliness he said, 'My brother is a fool with no manners, Capitan. His heart speaks before his head. What he means to say is that nobody ever comes to Cordovada Island except ourselves, not from one year's end to another. Naturally we are surprised to see visitors. The Americanos will not come here on account of the rip tides and the Kanakas will not come because they say the island is haunted, sir. Did you not know that?' he inquired blandly, and his brown, big muscular hand fell easily to the worn hilt of a twelve-inch knife he carried at his waist.

'It is true, the island is *haunted*, Capitan,' the smaller Leon observed, staring hard at the pearler skipper who evidently impressed him, and pulling a fearful expression to match his solemn warning. 'My brother and I have often seen the apparition of the mad Spaniard.'

'Sometimes it takes the form of a waterspout,' Luis explained factually. 'But of course my poor brother is too full of superstitions,' he added, giving his brother another ugly look and at the same time placing a finger against his forehead to indicate the extent of Leon's intelligence. 'Are you diving here for pearl-shell, Capitan?'

'We're prospecting,' Jim cut in cautiously.

'It is deep here to prospect, sir. Ah, lord, it is deep! A man must have very good gear – and very good courage,' Luis said with his eerie grin. 'You know our old father was crippled in this very place,' he added with a manufactured sob in his thick throat. 'He dived down there, Capitan,' he said, pointing a finger into the shimmering blue by the hull of the schooner. 'He went too deep – too deep. The pressure took away the use of his legs—'

'And the apparition sent him crazy,' Leon added for good measure.

'He has never walked for fifteen years,' Luis continued, still vigilantly scrutinising every part of the schooner as though memorising all its fittings and dimensions. 'He talks yet about a wreck of coral, Capitan—'

'And the terrible spectre that guards its treasure!' Leon broke in again.

'Idiot! Fool!' Luis snarled at his brother, and gave the wretched fellow a nasty dig in the ribs with his elbow.

'What treasure?' Dirk asked quietly. 'Who has been talking about treasure in the wreck?'

'Oh, pay no attention to my stupid brother, Capitan. He takes after our poor accursed father,' Luis coolly informed the schooner men by way of explanation. 'He thinks there must be a treasure in every wreck. No, no, it is not gold we seek, we are just penniless fishermen who wish to borrow a little sugar and coffee. We have had nothing but water to drink and fish to eat for three days.'

'Jim, make up a bag of provisions for them. See what we can spare,' Dirk told his shipmate.

'A thousand thanks, Capitan,' Luis said with gentle pleasure. 'We also have been divers, you know, my brother and I,' he added, as though now fully prepared to impart deep confidences. 'We gave it up after the Japanese diver failed to return when the salvage company tried to refloat the big wreck on the north reef.'

'What happened to the Japanese diver?' Jim inquired, pausing uncertainly on his way to the galley amidships.

'He failed to return, sir,' Luis answered cheerfully. 'Some say the tide trapped him in a blowhole. All they hauled up was his airhose. Are there but the two of you aboard, Capitan?' the Chamorro asked, suddenly going off at a tangent. 'Where is the rest of your crew?'

'We have two other men. They went to take a look at the Japanese boat, in the ship's dinghy. You must have seen them go.'

'Ah, of course, we see them go,' Luis said, and his grin had become mechanical as though his thoughts were on other matters. 'We see them go sure enough as we approach the reef passage. We have been lying at anchor behind the pinnacle rocks to the south of the island. And you say there are just the four men in your whole crew, Capitan! And two of them away. Do not bother with the provisions, sir! We will eat them here,' he said, looking across at Jim.

Luis nodded quickly at his brother and both men suddenly moved like cats. Leon jumped forward and seized Jim's arms, and almost as part of the same motion Luis swiftly drew his knife and put it at Jim's throat.

Although the pearler skipper and his mate had recognised the

Chamorros as doubtful characters they were completely surprised by this vicious show of force. And when Dirk made a move to go to his shipmate's assistance Luis stopped him in his tracks with a cold warning.

'Do not try anything, Capitan, or your friend will die! It will be necessary for us to kill him.'

'Now what's this?' Dirk demanded angrily but warily. 'You can't be hoping to hijack our ship. What do you really want from us?'

'That is not for me to say, Capitan. There is another who will tell you. Cabeza!' Luis suddenly shouted at the top of his voice.

Jim, staring at the Chamorro's knife, wouldn't have made a move if he'd been able, and Dirk waited in wondering silence. Almost at once it become obvious why Luis had shouted and for whom. The Chamorro fishing boat was made fast alongside, and now there was a swift movement aboard. A figure appeared from under the half-deck and a man came quickly and urgently over the schooner's bulwarks with a long jungle knife in his lean desperate hand.

'Alimud Din!' Dirk said under his breath.

'Cabeza, you were right, there are but two of them aboard,' Luis told his self-imposed master. 'The other two are away on the Japanese wreck. The ship is in our hands.'

Just for an instant Alimud Din stood silent like a deadly dark image by the bulwarks. He was wearing just a ragged pair of khaki dungarees with a leather belt. He had no shirt and he was barefoot. The physical ordeal of his single-handed journey to Cordovada Island had left its mark on him. And more so, the terrible ebb and flow of his hopes and fears had written a message of warning in his face for any man. His cheeks were thinner, his cheek-bones pronounced, his eyes sunken and burning. His obsession was like a disease that must slowly devour him even as it drove him on. The crude duplicity of the Chamorro brothers was a pallid thing beside the enduring malevolence of this tragic evil-minded Moro. And as they faced each other again Dirk remembered what Gomez had once told him about this man. 'There can be no cure for such a one but fortune, no peace but death.'

'Watch them!' Alimud Din directed with an uncanny tense calm which at any instant could explode into fanatical violence. 'Call out if either moves an inch!'

All sorts of ideas were coursing through Dirk's mind, but with Jim menaced so closely by the Chamorro's knife there was nothing he could do but wait on events and hope for some better opportunity to seize the initiative. The possibility seemed far away because obviously Alimud Din had planned carefully to make the most of his meagre chances. He went swiftly aft to the saloon companion-way and vanished below.

The men on deck waited tautly. Neither Luis nor Leon was smiling any more, and they both seemed to know what they were at, as though Alimud Din had drilled them well in this routine. Then away astern Dirk caught sight of the ship's dinghy, with O'Hara and Gomez pulling leisurely, just rounding the bluff.

A moment later Alimud Din reappeared at the head of the saloon companion-way, and now his face was relaxed, if one could call it that, in one of his bitter cynical smiles. He was carrying a Winchester rifle and a ·44 Webley revolver seized from the *Jolo*'s small armoury. It hadn't taken the Moro long to find what he was after because no effort had been made to conceal the fire-arms. They were kept, with ammunition, in a cupboard in the little chart-room where Dirk and Jim worked out their sights, courses and distances. Alimud Din knew the layout of the schooner because he had been aboard at Tawan and very little must have escaped his sharp eyes.

'Ah, señor, now we are really masters of your ship,' he said, gazing at Dirk with a dark smiling confidence. 'Here, Luis,' he demanded of the elder Chamorro, 'can you shoot a revolver?'

'I am an excellent knife-thrower, cabeza. Shooting is much easier,' Luis replied with a show of ugly teeth as he eagerly accepted the revolver. He slipped his knife back into its sheath and waved the gun about with rather naïve enthusiasm.

'Take care or you will shoot your brother!' Alimud Din warned irritably. 'Leon, you take my bolo,' he added, and the younger Chamorro stepped away from Jim and picked up the Moro's long jungle knife.

Alimud Din looked astern. He had already noticed the approach of the dinghy, but it was still a long way off and making slow time against the set of the current. Threatened now by their own guns Dirk and Jim were helpless. There was no doubt that by his swift move in seizing the ship's fire-arms Alimud Din had made himself master of the *Jolo*. He turned again to speak to Dirk.

'Señor Rogers, Fate has made you a fool, a pawn in a game for greater stakes than you can share. I am sorry for you, señor, because your foolishness makes life a burden for you as my poverty has made mine. Somehow you escaped from the Sacred Well. I do not ask how. It does not matter, for I know it was Fate brought you here on my trail to Cordovada Island.'

'That's a simple way of looking at things,' Dirk commented watchfully.

'I have to be simple, señor,' the Moro said, 'because I want you to understand quickly what you have to do before your friends return. Once before I told you that my quest is as a duty before me. That is the truth,' Alimud Din went on in a voice that suddenly began to shake with the violence of a powerful repressed passion, as though his body imprisoned an evil genie that must break out of the flesh at any instant. 'The Cordovada fortune is mine by destiny. I reached here by a boat I stole in Koror. I was wrecked on the reef and cast ashore with nothing. It was my fate, señor. For these poor fishermen found me. They helped me. They were sent to be my allies.

'The chart I took from the sword showed me that my treasure lay in the lagoon, but when I learned from these men that the ancient wreck lay deeper than the bottom of the Sacred Well I thought Allah was making sport of me. It was unworthy of me, señor. For then your diving boat put into the lagoon and I realised my destiny was bound with yours to the end – to the end, señor. Fate had sent you. For it is you, Señor Rogers, who salvaged the sword, who must also salvage the treasure!'

'You would have been wiser to wait till we had treasure to show before you played your hand,' Dirk said bleakly, gazing into the

Moro's glittering eyes. 'The wreck lies deep. Who knows if the treasure is there? Or if a diver can ever reach it?'

'You are a fool! You are too blind to see!' Alimud Din spat out the words, angry that the tiniest doubt should worm into his golden convictions of success. 'It is written in the ancient script. It is foretold by wise men. Only an idiot could not be convinced that I, Alimud Din, will claim the treasure of Cordovada and restore the fortunes of my noble family!'

For answer to this wild assurance Dirk turned to the two Chamorros who were listening unperturbed to Alimud Din's outpourings. 'And you, Luis – and Leon?' the schooner skipper asked. 'Do you suppose you will get anything but trouble from following this man?'

'I have promised. They will be well paid,' Alimud Din interrupted angrily. 'They will have their shares.'

'As he was paid in the Sacred Well?' Jim demanded grimly with a nod of his head at Dirk.

'We will take our chances,' Luis said calmly, cocking his head to one side with a wily grin. 'We are so poor, sir, we would need very little to be a hundred times better off. Even if we lose our lives they are not worth much, especially my brother's.'

'See, you cannot drive any wedges between us,' Alimud Din shouted triumphantly at hearing Luis's rather tangled expression of allegiance to his cause. 'These men understand fate as I do. Out of our poverty we know each other. If we must we will kill. It is very simple now that we are masters of the ship with these guns. Oh, it was not difficult to fool you, Señor Rogers. Twice I have fooled you so easily. You are a great diver, señor, but too trusting. You are stupid, too stupid to understand the skills of treachery!'

'Not stupid enough to dive down to that wreck for you, even if my life depends on it,' Dirk said.

'But your life does not depend on it, señor,' Alimud Din said with a gentle smile. 'It is your friend's life that is at stake! See, how simple it is to persuade you. But indeed there is no need for persuasions. Fate wills it, señor. We are all carried on its tide. That is why you will dive.'

The Moro's expression changed savagely. He pointed the rifle at Jim. 'Seize him!' he shouted. 'Bind him – his legs and arms!'

The Chamorros took hold of Jim, and when Dirk made an instinctive movement Alimud Din pointed the rifle at his chest. 'Stay where you are, señor. If I have to kill you I will know that Fate willed it so, and then your friend must do the diving!'

Once again Dirk swallowed his feelings, deciding to wait on better opportunities, and inside a minute Jim was tied up with a heaving line that had been lying on the hatch-top.

'Take him forward. Put him in the bow behind the windlass, out of sight,' Alimud Din instructed his helpers, and as they carried out this task he turned again to the pearler skipper.

'Now, señor, you are free to walk about your ship. Go anywhere you wish, but stay on deck. You can jump overboard if you like and swim ashore, but if you do I will surely shoot your friend and throw him after you. When we have tamed these others of your crew you and your men will live forward in the fo'c'sle till the job is ended. We will live aft, with the guns on watch, and a hostage to shoot. You see, señor. Fate favours the clever ones.'

Dirk was looking astern where O'Hara and Gomez, pulling a little faster as they neared the ship, were less than a cable's length distant.

'You will not give any alarm,' Alimud Din added, now supremely confident of his ability to run matters his own way. 'Your men will see the fishing boat to tell them the Chamorro brothers are visiting you. Do not mention my name. They must both come aboard. We will need them to help raise the treasure.'

At this Alimud Din went swiftly forward into the schooner's bows. He gave some rapid instructions to Luis, then he dropped out of sight behind the windlass. Dirk knew Jim was there as well, with the Moro's gun watching him.

Luis and Leon came aft. The elder brother had carefully thrust the revolver out of sight in his waist-band, covered by his tattered shirt. Leon surreptitiously kept the bolo behind his back till he reached the after hold. Here he took up a position standing with his back against the mainmast yard-arm, the bolo laid in the folds of the stowed mainsail. Luis went right aft on to the poop by the ship's wheel, and Dirk waited by the port quarter.

'*Jolo*, ahoy!' It was O'Hara giving a hail as they brought the dinghy alongside the pilot ladder that was made fast by the quarter. Both he and Gomez shipped their oars and the Irishman gripped the pilot ladder and looked up into Dirk's strained face.

'Are ye all right there?' O'Hara roared, sweating and boisterous as a bull in an arena.

'Come aboard,' Dirk said. He gave a glance forward and he could just see the peering dark face of Alimud Din around the windlass warping-drum.

O'Hara's face rose over the level of the bulwarks and he stared suspiciously at Luis and Leon who were both looking idiotically innocent.

'These men are the Vajas brothers,' Dirk explained. 'They're the Chamorro fishermen who sometimes stay aboard the freighter wreck.'

'Ah, so that's who they are! We was wonderin' whose that old fishin' craft alongside o' ye might be. Anyhow we got the stuff,' O'Hara added, 'and a proper job we had lowerin' it down that wreck, man. The hull's as high above the reef as a block o' flats. Are ye sure everythin's all right. Where's Jim hidin' hisself—'

O'Hara broke off what he was saying. He had hoisted himself on to the bulwarks to come inboard and Gomez was standing up in the dinghy preparing to follow him up the pilot ladder. And at that instant they all became suddenly aware of a peculiar whistle of wind over the island. The day was still hot and brilliant and the sea breeze light, but when they looked shorewards above the bluff they saw palm-tops tossing violently. Then, as the wind-note heightened, a smoky pillar of moisture, tall as a great tree, appeared in the lagoon around the bluff. It was spinning like a top, whistling eerily and travelling swiftly towards the stern of the schooner, setting the waters heaving under it; and this wave motion raced ahead until abruptly the schooner began to heave and plunge at her moorings as though a leviathan were surfacing under her, and the sea boosted under her counter, jarring and banging the Chamorro fishing boat against the hull and tossing Gomez frantically in the little dinghy where he hung grimly on to the pilot ladder.

In those few moments, while this was happening, every man stood staring at the phenomenon, for a waterspout is not a common sight even to sailors, and this one appearing so dramatically in the lagoon seemed filled with forebodings.

'*It is the spectre!*' Leon Vajas wailed. 'It will send us all crazy!' he moaned shrilly. He seized his jungle knife and swung it aloft as though to defend himself against the advancing water column. But he had no need of his fright because, as abruptly as it had started, the wind-scream died away, the pillar of vapour collapsed and a hissing cloud of water swept across the *Jolo*'s stern.

'What is wrong there?' O'Hara shouted suspiciously when he saw the big knife in Leon's grip.

The Irishman's alert demand started a pandemonium of movement – and nothing went as the Moro had planned. Luis suddenly produced his revolver, waving it like a sword.

'Come inboard and bring your friend, big man!'

As a reply O'Hara made a tremendous dive on to the hatch-top, sprawling forward and his great reaching hands taking Leon's legs from under him. Luis fired a random shot meant for the Irishman. It struck the goose-neck of the main yard-arm and went ricocheting overboard with a whine of metal.

Dirk's immediate thought was for his shipmate, Jim Cartwright, trussed up behind the windlass in the bow, with Alimud Din holding a gun over him. Even before Luis's shot, as O'Hara dived off the bulwarks, the pearler skipper started racing forward.

A second shot from Luis whistled between the mainmast shrouds. Alimud Din had appeared, tense as a panther, up in the bow against the heel of the bowsprit where he had been kneeling out of sight. But despite all his threats and confidence, in this crisis he wasn't calm or deadly enough to carry out his plan. First he turned the rifle on Jim, then aware of Dirk rushing at him he hesitated a split second, changed his mind and decided on the skipper. But something was quicker than either of them – another

shot from Luis's revolver, never aimed at all but meant for Dirk. It struck Alimud Din in the breast.

The impact of the bullet made the Moro stagger as though he'd been struck a blow with a club. He reeled against the bow bulwarks and blood stained his chest as his life drained away. He had been mortally hit, but as Dirk reached him to seize the rifle he tried to raise the weapon. It slipped from his grasp and fell over the bows. The Moro make a weak lunge after it and there, where the bulwarks were low, he gasped as he lost his balance and fell headlong into the sea.

Luis had stopped shooting. The sight of Alimud Din dying by his shot had taken the fight out of him. O'Hara had Leon held down on the deck in his iron grip. Gomez's head was raised over the portquarter bulwarks viewing the whole scene with a frozen amazement. Everything had happened so fast, so violently, and what had happened was irrevocable.

Dirk leaned over the bows and gazed into the blue deeps of the glimmering lagoon. The Moro had gone. There was no sign of him at all.

The pearler skipper's next move was to take his sheath knife and cut his shipmate loose. Then, as Jim stretched his limbs and thankfully got to his feet, Dirk went down aft. Here the men were all still watching each other vigilantly. Gomez had meanwhile climbed inboard and O'Hara was still holding Leon on the deck. Luis no longer menaced anybody with the revolver. He was holding it loosely by his side.

As Dirk approached Luis greeted him with a hopeless gesture and showed his outsize teeth in a resigned grin. 'The game is over, Capitan. We cannot play without our king and I have shot him. It was an accident of course. I did not mean to kill the Moro. Actually I was shooting at you, Capitan. The Moro was mad, you know, but it made a change from fishing and starving to share his dreams for a little time.'

'You had better give me back my gun,' Dirk told him.

Luis shook his head. 'No, Capitan, I have no fancy to go to prison, and such a long way to Koror, and think of all the questions the Americanos will ask. My little brother would suffocate in prison, Capitan. I could not permit it when I have a gun in my hand.' Luis's strange smile went cold on his powerful plain face and he raised the revolver again, this time turning it in O'Hara's direction.

'Let my brother go, big man, and we will go too. It is best we go peaceably.' The Chamorro turned again to Dirk. 'The price of a gun is not worth a life, Capitan, and even I could not miss at this distance!'

Dirk nodded at O'Hara. 'Let him go. We want no more shooting. But understand, Luis, we must report all this when we get back to Kunjang.'

'Make that a long time, Capitan. Better still, never go back at all, like me and my brother. The mission will look after our dear old father and everyone else will think we have been lost at sea.'

O'Hara had allowed Leon to get to his feet and now the two tattered barefoot desperadoes backed slowly to the schooner's starboard side where their craft was made fast. Leon went over the bulwarks first and then Luis, grinning a farewell as his head disappeared.

Dirk was glad to see them go. He really had no case against them, and rather strangely he still felt no hostility, for Luis's philosophy was too primitive and cruel to contest, and in any case if Alimud Din had not aroused the latent evil in the two Chamorro brothers they would probably never have been any bother.

Soon they heard the fishing boat's engine cough and start to thump. The craft went astern and only then did the schooner men crowd to the bulwarks to watch the Chamorros leave. They continued watching until the fishing yawl passed outside the reef and brown sails were hoisted. It turned off the wind, running south.

With the Chamorros gone peace seemed to have returned to the lagoon and the island. For upwards of an hour they talked over what had happened and how it might affect their plans, but at the end of it all Dirk agreed with the others that they should press on in an attempt to break into the wreck, and leave any other complications until they returned to Kunjang.

First of all they got the case of dynamite aboard from the dinghy. Then Gomez, who was acting as ship's cook, set to work in the galley preparing a much-needed meal, Jim and O'Hara began laying out diving gear and Dirk himself turned his attention to the explosives salvaged from the freighter wreck.

He carried the box to a work-bench amidships, just forward of the mainmast, and carefully opened one of the containers. It was packed closely with cartridges of submarine blasting gelatine which appeared to be in first-class condition. There was also a reel of high-velocity detonating fuse, useful for cutting open decks, but it seemed to have deteriorated and looked dangerous. At a pinch Dirk might have tried the fuse if he had not possessed, in his salvage gear, a small exploder and a supply of electric detonators acquired when he had been breaking down a ferry-boat wreck in the mouth of the Piral River.

He set to work preparing a comparatively small charge with which he hoped to blast through the coral growth immediately over the main hatchway which, from his previous dive, he estimated was situated just forward of the galleon's mainmast.

First he prepared the primer cartridge, which would initiate the shot. He bored the cartridge with an aluminium pricker, inserted the electric detonator, which he had tested and found conducting, hitched the leading wires about the cartridge, cleaned the bare ends, attached them to the shot-firing cable and fitted the joint insulator. Then he built up the charge with more cartridges and made a neat waterproof parcel. His chief concern was that the electric detonators would fail under pressure because they were only tested to about sixty pounds per square inch.

They had a very late lunch, nicely dished up by Gomez, then about half an hour later Dirk got into his gear. Besides the familiar self-contained outfit with separate mouthpiece, divemask and double hose, they also had aboard the *Jolo* an outfit with a full facemask and a single hose – single because the demand valve and mushroom exhaust valve were built into one unit at the side of the mask. Dirk had bought it for deep pearling and difficult salvage jobs, and its excellence was that the full facemask allowed his mouth free and he was able to have telephone communication with the surface. The outfit could be used with swimfins or weighted boots, with high-pressure tanks or a surface air supply, according to the nature of the job.

He put on the same heavy-duty suit he'd worn on his first dive, and the twin seventy-cubic-foot tanks; then he slipped on the headband carrying the receiver–transmitter telephone unit and tested the circuit to the loud-speaker cabinet on the bench beside the diving ladder. His voice came over clear, so he completed his outfit with swimfins, belt, gauges and a diver's knife worn in a sheathband about his right knee. Then he drew on the full facemask and began breathing from his tanks.

Lastly Jim handed him a twenty-inch crowbar with claw and pick ends. He slipped his wrist through an attached thong. The additional weight of this tool would help carry him smoothly to the bottom. Jim was standing by the telephone cabinet, O'Hara was tending the lifeline which had a telephone cable inlaid. Gomez was watching the compressor and winch motors.

A little wind had sprung up since midday, setting a chop on the lagoon waters, but the schooner stayed very steady at her moorings. Dirk faced inboard and started going down the diving ladder, and as he did so he looked forward, past the *Jolo*'s port bow and, quite a long way off – about three hundred yards – he saw several glistening black backs rolling in the breeze-flecked waters.

'They look like whales,' he said to Jim over his telephone.

Jim looked ahead; then he picked up a pair of binoculars and studied the creatures.

'They're pilot whales,' he told his skipper.

Dirk nodded. 'All right, keep your eye on them,' he said. Pilot whales or blackfish, which never grew much above fourteen feet in length, were peaceable creatures, unlike their terrible cousins the grampuses or killers. In another few moments Dirk had disappeared beneath the surface, hooked his arm about the shotrope and, like a parachutist, stepped into the blue.

Chapter Twelve

At Thirty Fathoms

He had been descending just three minutes when his swimfins touched coral, and he discovered himself once again on the ghostly hulk of the *San Nicolas*. He remained where he was for a few moments, adjusting himself to the depth, and already the creeping cold infiltrating through his suit had become an invisible enemy.

He peered at his depth gauge in the claustrophobic gloom. It showed one hundred and ninety feet. He had added six atmospheres of pressure to his body in his slide to the wreck, and to withstand it he was drawing air at eighty-six pounds per square inch through his demand valve.

Resting on his knees, and with an arm about the shotrope anchored to the deck by the cement-loaded sinker drum, Dirk spoke on his telephone.

'On deck!'

'Topside here!' came Jim's pressure-distorted voice.

'I am on the bottom. Stand by!'

Looking forward the pearler skipper could distinguish the galleon's great windlass on the upper deck – simply because he knew the grotesque shape could be nothing other than the relic of a windlass. There would be another on the main deck below and one aft too. The mainmast stood less than three yards from him. Looking aft from it he could recognise details of the wreck's outline in the blue-grey fog – massive coralline bulwarks, the sheered stump of a mizzen-mast, deck ladders and, at the limit of his vision, the break of the quarter-deck like the rampart of a fortress in the sea. Down here in the shifting gloom objects got easily magnified and out of perspective.

Dirk took a deeper breath, let go of the shotrope and launched himself across the few feet to the mainmast. He gripped the icy pillar and looked keenly for signs to enable him to detect the structure of the deck beneath. After a moment's scrutiny he reaffirmed what he had suspected. In these early eighteenth-century galleons there was a space in the ship's waist known as the 'booms' where boats and spars were lashed. And below the booms was the main hatchway for loading cargo, stores and guns.

Dirk's plan was to blow a hole through the booms into the hatchway and so reach the main gun-deck from where he hoped to make his way aft to the stern quarters, and in this way avoid having to break through the successive decks of the built-up stern.

The pearler skipper began prodding the coral floor with his crowbar. Here were stag's horn, stony, organ-pipe, brain and stinging corals, disguised with swaying weeds, sea fans and anemones, and alive with oysters, sea urchins, crayfish, spider crabs and starfish.

The crowbar had little effect so Dirk wasted none of his valuable time.

'On deck! Send down the charge!'

He got a reply at once, then he spent the next few minutes waiting impatiently at the foot of the shotrope and wondering what on earth was keeping them on deck. He breathed as lightly as possible to conserve his air and, as he remained practically motionless in the undersea twilight, life began to stir around him, for the wreck had become both a refuge and a hunting-ground for marine creatures. He saw numbers of small octopuses drifting just above the coral floor, starfish and crabs on the move, passing clouds of fish and a bat-shaped whip ray in undulating nightmarish motion across the misty quarter-deck.

'Below there!' Jim's voice, like a message from the stars, cut into Dirk's frozen trance as he endured the penance of the slow-moving moments at the foot of the shotrope. 'The charge is coming down! Do you hear me?'

'I – hear – you,' Dirk muttered, and his lips felt like stale putty and were just about as difficult to manipulate. He gazed upwards, but he could see no surface, just a tantalising glow, arching like an Arctic dawn above him. And just then he felt a curious 'bump' on the shotrope which actually moved the cement-filled sinker drum a trifle. Seconds after this a sharp distinct report reached him as shock waves travelled fleetly through the fathoms. Chilled though he was, a deeper chill traversed Dirk's nerves like iced lightning.

'On deck! What has happened?'

'It's that school of whales,' came Jim's instant reply. 'They've been around us. O'Hara fired a rifle shot to scare them off!'

Now Dirk realised what had caused that queer 'bump' on the shotrope. A pilot whale had tripped the rope with a fluke or a flipper; but this thought was as nothing to his concern about O'Hara's rifle shot. A trickle of sweat broke out on his brow, cold as the sea around him.

'On deck! Jim! Do you hear me?'

'I hear you.'

'Stop that shooting! No more shooting! Do not fire again,' Dirk said slowly and tensely. 'The dynamite – *it might detonate!*'

Shock waves travel powerfully in water and the reverberations of a rifle shot could easily explode a submerged charge in the vicinity. However, some moments later, Dirk was relieved to see the charge of blasting gelatine appear. It had been placed in a perforated bucket which had been shackled to the shotrope so that it would not run adrift. Dirk removed the charge with its trailing firing cable, launched himself to a ragged hole he had made in the coral just forward of the wreck's mainmast and there he carefully laid the charge, covering it with some slabs of loose coral.

A check on his pressure gauge showed he had used all of one tank and was starting on his second. Seventy cubic feet of air had gone and he'd been below just twelve minutes. This was because he had been resting part of the time; a free swimming diver would use on average about seven cubic feet of air a minute at thirty-two fathoms deep, and, of course, after a considerable stay at such a depth he would need a correspondingly long period of decompression on his ascent.

'On deck! All's well. Bring me up!'

Dirk slipped an arm about the shotrope as his lifeline tightened and O'Hara started hoisting him, which was very easy since his emptying tanks were giving him a positive buoyancy. Quickly the grey gloom of the *San Nicolas* sank away beneath him.

Meanwhile, Jim and Gomez were activating the decompression system Dirk planned to use, and when the pearler skipper reached a depth of about ten fathoms he found an iron grating waiting for him, lowered from the ship, with an airhose seized to one of its spans and carrying a non-return valve attachment.

Dirk gripped the grating, thankful for the warmth and light of these blue shining waters below the *Jolo*'s keel, and he manoeuvred himself on to it.

'I'm on the stage. Turn on the air!' he directed over his telephone.

Between the reducing valve and the demand valve of his breathing equipment there was a hook-up or coupling for an airhose, an arrangement known as a demand surface supply. And when air started bubbling from the surface hose he engaged the coupling, shut off his high-pressure tanks and commenced breathing directly from the surface air, which was supplied from a reservoir attached to the compressor motor.

Some thirty minutes later, after finishing his decompression, Dirk was brought up on the grating from his last stage, and he came aboard, removed his mask and felt the sunshine on his face.

'What was the idea, firing a rifle shot when we've got a hundred-weight of dynamite aboard and a charge keeping me company down in the lagoon?' he demanded, looking accusingly from Jim to O'Hara.

'Oh, I'm beggin' your pardon for that, skipper! It wasn't Jim's fault at all, y'know,' O'Hara said with an expression of sincere regret. 'When I seen them whales plungin' around the shotrope I just slipped below for the rifle and niver thinkin' o' the danger I just let off a round to scare them brutes!'

'If you scared them half as much as you did me they won't stop running till they cross the Line!' Dirk said with a consoling grin.

There was a bit of a growing swell in the lagoon, working across from the direction of the churning reef passage, like some endless monster coiling under the surface, and the *Jolo* kept up a slight but constant movement, tightening and easing her bow cables like a horse testing the strength of its tethers. It was mid-afternoon, warm and breezy, with sunshine coming between the clouds in long brilliant intervals. Ashore the tall palms on the higher parts of the island swayed restlessly.

'I don't like the look of the weather,' Jim remarked. 'It's worsening slowly but surely.'

On this warning note they made preparations to fire the first shot without delay. Jim connected up the firing leads to the exploder, a magneto type housed in an aluminium casing and, for safety's sake, actuated by a plunger with considerable resistance. It was not necessary to shift the schooner for so small a charge at such a depth and, at a signal from Dirk, Jim thrust the plunger home. For several moments nothing seemed to happen, then there came a muffled thud on the ship's bottom. That was all.

Dirk had not planned to risk another dive that day, but the firing of the first shot had gone so smoothly and, after a break for tea, the light was still so good, he decided to go down to satisfy his curiosity about the effect of the blast.

He was soon ready and in addition to his other gear he was burdened still further this time by a battery underwater lamp worn above his facemask, so it would shine directly where he was facing.

Within a few minutes he was under water and on his way down the shotrope. He made a quick uneventful descent and it was just four o'clock in the afternoon when his swimfins touched the coral deck of the *San Nicolas* once more. In lots of ways conditions were adverse but strangely enough he felt he could see much better this time. Perhaps because he was beginning to find his environment familiar, like a dreamer dreaming the same nightmare several times in succession.

He informed Jim that he had touched bottom, then he left the shotrope, closed with the mainmast and examined the upper deck where he had laid his charge. His spirits rose when he found a jagged black hole at least six feet in circumference. The upper deck was open and the way clear into the main deck below.

'On deck! I am entering the wreck. Give me all the slack I need.'

He switched on his lamp, and gazed into the black pit in the wreck beside which the grey twilight on deck seemed almost companionable, then gripping his crowbar he allowed himself to sink downwards.

Firstly his yellowish lamplight illuminated the blackened oak beams of the booms, which had survived his explosive charge. The coral had been blasted down and he discovered it lying just six feet below in pulverised heaps. Dirk came to a rest on the greasy planking of the ship's main deck. He rested more or less on his knees and he turned himself about, discovering the mainmast again, descending through the deck levels, and an open hatchway, surrounded by a rail, and a stairway leading deeper.

It was as he had suspected, the interior of the vessel was open, for the outside coating of coral had prevented any growths within. The sea in the interior was profoundly cold and deadly still, but fortunately it was remarkably clear and his lamplight showed him a little more than he had expected.

Dirk hauled down fathoms of lifeline and telephone cable, coiling it with elaborate slow-motion caution, and finding it terribly difficult to keep himself from drifting up under the deckhead. When he had enough line he made a bight fast to the rail about the hatchway. Paying out this line would be easier than dragging it behind him, and he would be able to haul himself back by it to the hole in the deck.

He turned aft, swimming under the deckhead, and keeping to the port side so he could keep track of his progress. There was wreckage on this deck, most of it barely recognisable – crates, barrels, broken windlass bars, furniture, rotting bales, and at intervals he would negotiate the bulk of a muzzle-loading cannon, cemented now to its pad where it had been racked down on its tackles two centuries ago. Then his progress ceased, because he found the six-foot deck space jammed with an indescribable confusion of debris and amidst it all the hulks of cannon, which must have broken loose in the ship's last plunge and run berserk until they finally lodged in this brutal mass of rusting, twisted, crushed wreckage barring the pearler skipper's progress.

Dirk rested close to the deck, one hand gripping a slimy spar. Above the hoarse intake of his demand valve and the tinny squeak of his exhaust he had become conscious of a liquid 'creak' within the wreck as though in some uncanny fashion it were alive; and in those few moments he felt suddenly oppressed by the incredible unreality of his situation – the first man for centuries to breathe between these aged decks! Just then it seemed fantastic, just a fairy-tale, that this gruesome hulk had ever been buoyant on the surface, feeling the wind, resounding with commands and human action. And then, as though to underline his forebodings, his light beam glimmered awesomely on scattered bones beside an over-turned cannon.

There was no way past that wall of ruin where, amidst the terror and panic of sinking, loose cannon running amok on the main deck had made a chaos only quenched by the inundating sea. Dirk screwed himself about, bumping his tanks metallically on the deck-head beams. Better first to explore the lower decks in the hope of finding a clear run through the stern quarters, even if it meant having to go deeper into the bowels of the ship. He had only a few yards to swim back to the hole he'd blasted but it took him what seemed a lifetime as he laboriously groped his way back on his lines.

'Below there!' came Jim's voice, down through the pressing fathoms, into the darkness of the wreck. 'Are you all right?'

'All's well,' Dirk answered jerkily. He had no mind to waste breath on conversations. Then he tried switching out his lamp and he found he could see the pale ocean-bed light glimmering through the hole in the upper deck. When at length he arrived back under the booms he was surprised to learn from his luminous watch

that he had been no more than ten minutes on the wreck. If he had accomplished anything at all it was in a negative sense, so he decided to enter the lower gun-deck, for he had tested his surface airhose system on his previous dive and he meant to rely on it for his decompression.

'On deck! I need more slack. I am going into the lower deck!'

So he began hauling down several more fathoms of slack on his lines, which he estimated he must need if he was to reach the stern by way of the lower deck. Then he made another hitch to a ladder rail, with fingers like frozen sticks, switched on his lamp and dropped over the hatch coaming into the blackness of the galleon's lower gun-deck.

There was even less headroom down here. A tall sailor must have had to walk and work with his head stooped or brain himself on the deckhead beams. And Dirk found his difficulties verging on the impossible as he struggled aft, half swimming, half dragging himself, his lines ever entangled in his swimfins. One moment his lamp and tanks would be scraping and bumping under the deckhead, the next his face would be brushing the deck planking. However, as he struggled along the port side he found the lower deck reasonably clear. He kept negotiating cannon which glimmered like robot monsters in his lamp beam and between each were the pathetic remains of sea chests, bottles, bags, platters, mugs, helmets, knives and cutlasses, tools, even petrified hats and boots and clothing and, worst of all – enough to shake the confidence of an explorer anywhere, much less thirty fathoms deep inside a wreck – occasional skeletons of the crew!

Dirk went on by the foot of the mizzen-mast, past a stern capstan, another hatchway, and at last found his passage barred by a bulkhead. He turned along it until his lamp revealed the hinges and ring handle of a narrow door, bearing a metal coat of arms, long since corroded beyond translation. There were no bolts on this side and the door seemed as immovable as rock. Dirk realised it would be a long job breaking it open with hand tools, but a light charge would probably do the trick. Just one cartridge set in the door centre.

He made a tortuous journey back to the main hatch under the booms and on the way he decided that on his next trip he must abandon swimfins and wear weighted boots. It was the only way to make any progress down here. With almost as much relief as if he'd reached the surface he eventually found himself standing in open water on the galleon's upper deck, close by the mainmast.

He had reached the shotrope and was about to give the order for them to haul him up when he chanced to peer down aft. He could see dimly beyond the stump of the mizzen-mast to the old fossilised ship's wheel on the quarter-deck, and it seemed to the pearler skipper that a human figure was standing behind it!

'Below there! Are you ready to come up?'

Dirk looked at his pressure gauge. He was nearly down to emergency level. There was scarcely more than enough to reach first-stage level.

'Haul up!' he said.

That night, over their evening meal, Dirk told the others what he had discovered below, about the bulkhead door which barred any further progress and which he hoped to blow with a light charge first thing next morning. Oddly enough, he did not mention the 'figure' he had seen beside the ship's wheel. Now that he was back on deck the idea seemed ridiculous, a touch of narcosis, an underwater aberration, the sort of thing he had often warned Jim to guard against.

After writing up his log and diary Dirk turned into his bunk early, leaving his shipmates to split the anchor watches between them, for he needed rest if he were to make more hard deep dives. He lay down as a squall swept the schooner's decks, setting her rocking at her cables, and he hoped rough weather was not going to keep them chafing idly at the anchorage.

As it turned out weather conditions were not very good next morning. There was some sunshine and the temperature stayed high but the monsoon weather had come to stay, bringing frequent rain squalls out of the wind's eye. North-westerly was not a kindly slant for Cordovada Island because it sometimes carried the long 'scend' of Pacific rollers right across the reef flat, making the lagoon foam and boil like an overfilled cauldron. However, Dirk decided to continue; he had dived in much worse conditions.

First of all he prepared a light charge for blowing the aft bulkhead door, then straight after breakfast he got into his diving gear, but this time he made some important changes in his equipment. Instead of swimfins he wore a pair of brass-soled diving boots which would keep his feet on the bottom; and instead of carrying the big 'seventy' tanks, which he'd found so cumbersome between the low decks of the wreck, he had decided to go all the way on a surface airhose hooked up to his demand valve. As a safeguard, and solely for an emergency, he carried one small thirty-five-cubic-foot tank, on which he could reach the surface if his airhose failed or got fast.

It was breezy when he went down the diving ladder and the schooner's hull was lifting and falling two or three feet in the lagoon swell. Foam from the ship's stem swept across his divemask before he submerged. Then he gripped the surging shotrope and made a good descent.

His first task when he reached the wreck this morning was to shift the sinker so that the shotrope ran straight down through the main hatchway and, with some hoisting and lowering, and a little heaving and veering on the schooner's moorings, he got this job done. As he worked he could hear his boots crunching in the coral and see them raising puffs of debris and weed. He breathed with reasonable comfort from the surface airhose.

This first task completed, Dirk telephoned for the charge to be sent down and, as he stood by the shotrope, awaiting the arrival of the perforated bucket, he peered about with more attention. Visibility wasn't very good but he could see as far as the ship's wheel on the quarter-deck – and he stiffened instinctively – because that morbid figure was still there.

At that moment he was warned of the arrival of the blasting charge. The gelatine cartridge was a pressing urgency, so he removed the charge from the bucket and sank into the black well in the wreck, down through two decks to the lower gun-deck. Then, feeling more able and efficient in his boots, he turned aft and ploughed along the sea-drowned gun-deck, paying out his lines, his footsteps like doom itself in the ancient hulk. He managed much better this time in his sixteen-pound boots, with no need to worry about running out of air, and at length his lamp beam showed him the bulkhead door. With customary caution he set the explosive charge, then he followed his lines back to the main hatch.

This time, as he came hand over hand up the shotrope to the twilit vista of the galleon's upper deck, he looked aft very deliberately and warily. And this time he was sure he was not suffering from narcosis. This time he was positive a figure was standing behind the ship's wheel – *the figure of a man!*

Dirk hesitated a few seconds then, knowing he had no need to worry about expending air, he started going aft. It wasn't far really, just a few slow-motion steps to the break of the poop, a deep breath to lift himself gropingly up the overgrown deck ladder; then he was on the sloping quarter-deck, abaft the mizzen-mast stump. There was only the sound of his own heaving breaths, and the squeal of his exhaust air flighting surfacewards, and the fearsome cold gnawing at his hands, and that green-hued, bloated, human figure by the galleon's steering-wheel in the gelid deeps!

Dirk stared grimly from behind his divemask at this most gruesome find of all on the galleon wreck. For minutes now he had realised it was the body of Alimud Din. Here the Moro was, a lifeless corpse, carried by submarine currents to lodge with an evil irony against the wheel of the treasure ship he had been so ruthless to find. His body was trapped in this grotesque upright attitude by the sharp coral fangs on the wheel, his hair drifting loose like weed.

Dirk reached out a hand and gave the pathetic corpse a push. It broke loose and began to drift slowly across the quarter-deck, passing through the shattered bulwarks and, as the pearler skipper started back to the shotrope, it vanished in the gloom of the lagoon floor.

It was upwards of forty-five minutes later when, his staging completed, Dirk was brought aboard the *Jolo*, and as he drank a cup of coffee to thaw out his chilled limbs, he told his surprised shipmates what he had seen that morning, and what had been the end of Alimud Din and his crazy desires.

'When he went overboard he must have gone straight down under our keel,' Jim commented.

'The Moro believed in fate,' Gomez said, placing a hand on his breast, 'and fate was true for him. It brought him to his treasure ship, but he was never to know it himself!'

After some little more discussion Jim went to connect the firing-cable leads to the exploder, with O'Hara assisting him.

'Here's hoping it really is a treasure ship,' Jim said feelingly as he worked.

'And here's hopin' there's nothin' else but treasure in it,' O'Hara muttered darkly.

'What d'you mean?' Jim demanded.

'Maybe those simple Chamorros are more right than us clever ones,' O'Hara brooded. 'Wind and water the spectre may be, but it seems to have a mighty tight grip o' the gold! Look what happened to that thievin' Moro!'

'Don't you start talking like that to the skipper,' Jim warned the big Irishman. 'He has enough to worry about besides superstitions!'

The weather was slowly deteriorating and just as they were finishing the job a squall hissed across the lagoon, deluging the schooner and its crew, and Jim had to throw a tarpaulin over the firing gear. For ten minutes the wind screamed, then the turmoil of rain sped southwards, and quite suddenly a bright hot flush of sunshine swept over the island.

A minute later Jim pumped the exploder plunger. They listened tensely; but the charge was deep within the wreck, and there was only the sound of the sea and the wind and the gulls calling.

'The meter showed a reading,' Jim said. 'The charge has gone off all right. Haul in the firing cable, O'Hara!'

The cable came in freely, with no entanglements, and after a time O'Hara drew in the bare end where it had been severed by the shot. By this time they were all ready for their midday meal and then, an hour or so later, Dirk began to prepare for his second dive that day, his most important one, he hoped.

Chapter Thirteen

The Treasure

This time the *Jolo*'s skipper went straight down on the shotrope until he reached the lower gun-deck of the wreck. As before he hauled down enough slack on his lines to take him all the way to the stern; then he followed his spearing lamp beam under the low deckhead tracing his way, step by step, till he reached the bulkhead.

Even in these morbid oppressive surroundings he felt a flush of elation when he saw that the bulkhead door was shattered. He kicked away some loose timber, then stepped through into a middle passage-way. He struggled on, following the haunting glow of his lamp, dragging his lines astern of him, his boots and equipment bumping and scraping against waterlogged timbers, his exhaust air rustling and booming in the tight confinement.

Minutes passed as, almost with a mindless feeling, Dirk inspected cramped compartments in the ship's hull on either side of the passage-way, and he recognised timber beds, cupboards and chests, stools and crockery, even a metal lantern still suspended from the deckhead. Then he stumbled into an armoury with racks still loaded with rusting pikes, axes and cutlasses. And there were stacks of powder kegs, ropes, chains and tackles, all black, rotting and corroding.

The skipper pushed on, staggering over steering chains to the foot of a deck ladder leading from aloft. Alongside this ladder, all within the space of a few steps but a mystifying maze in the black

sea-filled wreck, he found another low door. It was open – jammed
back, no doubt by a flood of water from above.

Dirk knew he was about as far aft as he could get, almost to the
rudder post, but he knew also he was where he must expect to find a
lazaret or bullion chamber. The ghostly eye of his lamp revealed a
compartment showing the great skeletal frames, trestles and knees
of the stern structure. And here were stacked several large boxes.
He attacked one of these with his crowbar. The metal clasps
crumbled and he levered off the lid. To his surprise the box was
packed with muskets. He was disappointed but the presence of
these valuable weapons confirmed his opinion that this stout compartment in the stern was a place of security. It must lie directly
under the commander's stateroom. What better place could there
be in a ship for bullion . . .?

Like some aquatic monster in his eerie rig, with his staring electric eye, his exhaust bustling under the lowering beams, counting
time by his harsh breath intakes, Dirk surveyed the frigid chamber.
He noticed a grey-green glimmer on the deck and stooping he
found a human skull . . . then the rest of a skeleton, the remnants of
leather sea-boots, a belt and a dagger. There was another skeleton
close by, and yet another in a sitting position against the ship's side.
These men must have been overwhelmed by a flood of water from
above.

Suddenly one of Dirk's booted feet sank into nothingness, and to
retain his balance he went down on his knees. Now his lamp
showed him a well in the deck and an open trapdoor! The well was
not deep, perhaps less than three feet, a hidden compartment
within a compartment. And on the edge of the well, beside the
trapdoor, there was a blackened aged chest, hooped with metal,
about eighteen inches long and twelve deep and wide. Below in the
well there were other chests. Dirk counted five more.

He turned his attention to the chest which the drowned men had
apparently secured from the well before they were overwhelmed.
He put a bight of his lifeline about it and found he could move it
with a reasonable effort. With his crowbar he broke the padlocks
which were corroded to a paper thinness, and he turned back a

curving lid which groaned protestingly in the gloomy lazaret. And there, within inches of his divemask, was what he was searching for – stacks of closely-packed gold coins, yellow in his lamp beam, a fortune in Spanish gold. Here, at last, thirty fathoms deep, was the treasure of Cordovada!

Dirk took just one coin as proof of his success, then he pushed back the lid. Getting these six chests to the surface must wait for another day. He was just about to telephone his good news to the *Jolo* when he was startled by a suspicious shudder that passed right through the ship. Moments later an uncanny weight of water humped aft into the lazaret, bringing a slight squeeze of pressure as though something huge had moved within the wreck. At that same instant – doubtless because of the pressure increase – his lamp went out with a startling thud! It was below the depth it had been designed for anyway, and now the sea weight had crushed it.

He was left in a darkness that only seemed to have been waiting to engulf him as it had done the wretched mariners two centuries ago!

Dirk stayed on his knees for a while in the freezing blackness, trying to detect above the sound of his air some clue to that threatening shiver in the wreck's structure; then warily he got to his feet and began groping along his lifeline, more precious now than gold, the thread that could lead him out of this submarine catacomb back to light and life.

'Below there!'

It was a voice in his ear, Jim's voice within the wreck, more astonishing than if it had been from another world.

'Are you all right?'

'I have – found – the gold!' Dirk said in a numbed hoarse whisper. 'My lamp – is out. I am – moving back – to the shotrope!'

He turned to face forward and he began threading his way back, feeding the tough lifeline towards him, step by step, keeping his head down to avoid the beams, and when he had struggled through the bulkhead door shattered by his explosive he saw a glow of light ahead, shafting down through the hole in the upper deck like pallid moonbeams. There were flashes of silver in the beams where a few fish were circling.

When Dirk reached the main hatchway he unhitched his lines and telephoned the *Jolo* again. They hauled in the slack and in a minute more he was on his way up, his heart lightening as the wreck vanished beneath him and the thought of his success began to excite him.

'Why, skipper, it's a bloomin' divil diver ye are to be sure, man!' O'Hara roared joyously when, nearly an hour later, Dirk was telling his shipmates about the wealth he had found below. 'Mind ye,' the Irishman added, 'I always swore ye'd find that gold, but to tell the truth I thought I was making a liar out of meself!'

'The stuff is down there all right – six chests of it,' Dirk assured him with a chilly grin as he gratefully accepted a steaming mug of coffee from Gomez.

'Did you see the gold pieces with your own eyes?' the Filipino demanded.

Dirk nodded and his stiff fingers probed in his belt and he produced a single gold coin in the palm of his hand. 'There it is, Gomez – Cordovada's gold!'

Gomez gazed at the coin wonderingly, then he passed it into O'Hara's eager hand.

'Bless me unworthy soul,' the Irishman said in a whisper. 'It's half choked I am to be holdin' it – all the way from two hundred feet under the ocean!'

'All the way from two hundred years ago as well,' Jim reminded him.

That night they spent rather restlessly with the solitary gold piece of Cordovada's treasure aboard the *Jolo* and the wreck, two hundred feet deep, still guarding the rest.

Morning came with a fresh wind rising, cloudy skies and a roughish sea that spread the edges of its temper into the lagoon. These were poor conditions for diving but Dirk was anxious now to get the job finished, not least because he had become oppressed on his last dive by the fateful atmosphere in the wreck. He was not superstitious, but it would have needed a very unnatural temperament not to be affected by working where he had made such grim finds.

Jim, sensing his skipper's feelings, suggested he should share the diving, but Dirk turned down the notion. He reckoned it would be unprofitable for Jim to start learning his way into the wreck at this stage and besides, he was of the opinion it wasn't right to send his partner where he was not keen on going himself.

So by eight o'clock that morning Dirk had entered the lagoon with his mind geared to the decision of raising all six chests that day. He estimated that he could manage this task in three dives, with a bit of luck. Instead of manhandling the chests he meant to use winch power and his plan was to take a derrick runner straight down through the main hatchway, then turn it along the lower gun deck by a snatch block stropped to the mainmast foot. By telephone he could keep a close control on the winch and the chests could be hauled along the lower gun-deck to the hatchway.

Dirk used the same diving gear as on the previous day, except that he carried another underwater lamp, an older type with a do-it-yourself pressure casing, and apart from the few expected snags all went remarkably well and by early afternoon all this hard work had been accomplished in two long dives. All that remained was to winch the bullion chests in a straight lift to the surface from the hole in the waist of the wreck, and it was four o'clock that day when Dirk stepped into Cordovada lagoon for the last time.

All day the wind had been freshening and now it was putting a moan into the *Jolo*'s rigging, and at times the schooner would lift sharply with a sudden swell under her bows only to be checked by her straining moorings, and she would shake unsteadily.

The mainmast derrick was closely guyed and its runner, hook and sling sagged over the grey-green sea, its hauling part carried to the warping-drum of the schooner's winch, manned by Gomez – a Gomez whose urgent desire for Spanish gold seemed to have got jaded by his concern for his skipper's safety. O'Hara, rugged as granite, stood by the head of the diving ladder, tending Dirk's lines, the wind fluttering his curly hair and tattered shirt.

Jim, by the loud-speaker telephone, looked grimy and worn, his keen hard eyes scanning everything – the sea, the sky, the lagoon, the ship's moorings, the derrick gear and the diving equipment.

Dirk was standing straddle-legged by the diving ladder, a tall ominous figure in his heavy-duty suit, solid boots, full facemask and hood. He checked his telephone to Jim; his valves for the thirty-five-cubic-foot tank on his back; then the flow of air from the ship's compressor reservoir being fed direct to his demand valve. All was working correctly, and the compressor engine was thudding stolidly abaft the mainmast to leeward. He went down the ladder and the green swell gushed up the ship's hull to meet him, boosting over his shoulders. In another moment he was submerged with the surface churning over his head. He gripped the shotrope, and began his long slide to the wreck.

He made the descent in good time, finding visibility poor because of the cloud on top. The wreck had no colours except forlorn blues and greys marked by heavy shadows. On his way down there had been a surprisingly strong current, even near the bottom of his dive, and he guessed the stiff seas beyond the reef were pouring through gaps as submarine waterfalls and stirring up the whole lagoon.

'On the bottom!' he reported into his transmitter, and looked about to get his bearings. He had descended right through the main hatchway to the lower gun-deck and he found the six bullion chests at his feet.

'Send down the runner!'

His boots thudded on the deck planking as he manoeuvred a chest into position. His intention was to hoist them one at a time, and so avoid the risk of losing more than one if there should be an accident. Soon the runner hook and sling slipped down the hatchway and, on his knees, Dirk hauled the sling under the chest with icy fingers and carried it back under the safety spring on the hook.

'Hoist away!'

He watched fascinated, with a sense of achievement, as the first of the bullion chests was hoisted slowly from the hatchway, then vanished rapidly in the green mist above. After that it seemed just a matter of routine – terse telephone directions, the arrival of the hook and sling, and another chest's departure. Two – three – four, soon a fortune was stacked on the *Jolo*'s decks, and as Dirk watched the fifth chest disappear he felt a joyful rise of spirits that momentarily made him forget the numbing cold gripping his limbs. Now it all seemed so easy, with all the hard work behind and just one more chest to hoist.

It was then, as if timed to quell his enthusiasm, that he was dismayed to feel a shudder run through the wreck. This time he felt a definite movement in the deck, accompanied by a slow creak of timber under strain.

He waited . . . seconds passed . . . and nothing more occurred, but he could feel the uneasy aftermath of heavy currents spreading into the wreck. The lagoon was astir today with big seas riding across the northerly reefs. Two long minutes dragged by, then he heard from the surface again. They had boarded the fifth chest and the hook was running down.

Dirk waited grimly, watching impatiently for the hook and sling to appear. Then a second time the wreck shivered. The deck shifted inches under his feet and the groan of timber was carried to a horrifying breaking-point! Dirk's breath came faster. He couldn't afford to give himself another minute down here!

Then he saw the hook and sling sailing down on the runner. He had the last chest ready and waiting. Tensely he went through the familiar motions – hauling the bight of the sling under and over, and making it fast behind the hook safety spring.

'*Hoist away!*' he said urgently into his transmitter.

Chapter Fourteen

Fast!

Aboard the *Jolo* there was not now much semblance of tropical weather. The wind was keen as a razor in the schooner's rigging and a rain squall had just drenched ship and men alike. 'White horses' were running on the rollers outside the reefs, clouds of spray were boosting through coral blowholes, and a nagging swell made sword-like ridges on the lagoon surface, chewing and thudding against the schooner's hull. Ashore the palms were tossing, the cliffs looked grey and the coves were desolate as moon craters.

'Hoist away!' Jim suddenly roared at Gomez who was standing at his post by the winch, and the sharp little Filipino opened the throttle and the derrick runner came churning in, wet and hard on his hands.

'This is the last o' them and thank heaven for it!' O'Hara said with a savage glance at the black sodden chests standing on the deck amidships. 'I've suffered as much dread o' this cursed place as if I'd been hauntin' it meself!'

His words were lost in the wind but somehow the other two knew what was in the Irishman's mind and they were smiling with relief and anticipation when suddenly the shotrope jerked rigid as an iron bar! The strain took the schooner over until her port-side scuppers flooded; then the rope began to strand, like toffee stretching, until it parted with a soft thud and the schooner swung back sharply on to an even keel.

'Stop heaving!' Jim yelled.

Gomez stopped the winch and took a turn on the drum with the runner.

'D'ye see what has happened? The shotrope has carried away!' O'Hara cried emotionally, and he turned in fierce concern to Jim who was grim and pallid and suddenly looked years older. The young mate spoke huskily into the telephone transmitter.

'Below there! Are you all right?'

The wind shrilled; there was a grey rain squall advancing from beyond the reef, and the schooner creaked dismally at her moorings; but there was no answer from the blank dialled face of the loud-speaker telephone cabinet. It was alive no longer. It was just a box, inanimate, dead.

'Below there! Dirk! Do you hear? Do you hear?'

There was no answer from the green depths. As priceless seconds raced past O'Hara and Gomez rushed to the ship's bulwarks and stared as though paralysed into the heaving, grumbling, aggressive lagoon waters. What was happening all those fathoms below? And then, as if to underline the terror of some unknown tragedy, about fifty yards astern, gouts of air began blowing up!

Gomez swung about, gazing helplessly at Jim Cartwright. 'In heaven's name, señor – what can have happened?'

'We – we must have fouled the shotrope with the runner,' Jim began, then he stopped desperately. 'No – it must be more than that. He doesn't answer – and all that air!' he gasped, looking astern, where quantities of air were still bubbling to the surface.

'Where is that goddam air coming from – his hose or his tank?' Gomez exclaimed wide-eyed with anxiety.

'Heave in on his lines!'

O'Hara instantly began heaving in the dripping airhose and lifeline. They came freely, hand over hand, fathom after fathom, and seemed to be leading from astern.

'God help him!' the Irishman groaned with a crack in his growling voice. 'He has broken adrift altogether!'

'Keep a sharp look out astern!' Jim said urgently. 'If he throws off his boots and weights he can surface on his tank supply. Without a shotrope he'll drift a long way astern.'

Jim gave a glance forward, over the schooner's see-sawing bows, beyond the reefs where a mile-high curtain of rain was storming towards the lagoon. He started dragging off his shirt, shoes and dungarees. 'I've got to get down there – quick!' he said between his teeth.

Just wearing his trunks – there was no time for a suit – the schooner mate seized the emergency twin-tank diving set lying ready charged by the main hatch coaming. Gomez jumped to help him on with the gear with trembling, hasty hands, and it was then the rain squall hit the boat. The decks disappeared in inches of white water; the lagoon swell was crushed in the hissing downpour; the wind rose to a scream in the schooner's rigging; and the world about the vessel contracted to walls of driving rain.

Jim struggled on with his gear, scarcely able to see his companions in the deluge. Swimfins dragged on – harness buckled – weight belt latched – mask pulled on – and lastly, the mouthpiece. He turned on his air and started breathing from his tanks, and he was at the head of the diving ladder when O'Hara shouted at him.

'Ye cannot swim down all that way, man! Besides ye'll niver find the wreck without a shotrope. The current will carry ye miles away!'

'The derrick runner!' Gomez cried, pointing to where the runner dipped and swayed in the lagoon close by the ship's side. 'That last chest is no more than half-way up. I'll slip it back on the wreck. It will surely not run adrift!'

Jim nodded as he moulded his divemask about his temples. Already the rain squall was driving past. The island shores and the reefs were taking shape again. . . .

He did not bother with the diving ladder. He jumped feet first into the lagoon from the poop deck – surfaced – looked for the derrick runner – found it just an arm's length away, wrapped his legs about it and before O'Hara had given Gomez the signal to run down on the winch Jim had vanished under the surface, hauling himself down, hand under hand.

As the young mate descended, Gomez began to run the bullion chest back on to the wreck – it was heavy enough not to go adrift in the strongest of currents – and Jim's downward slide was accelerated. He went down rapidly, drawing the apparently endless line from beneath, and for a little while he glimpsed those horrifying blasts of air rushing to the surface, then there was nothing but the grey sea around him.

Dirk was watching the last chest sail into the green ceiling above him when once again he experienced that threatening shudder in the bones of the wreck and chilling groan of timber under strain.

At once he gripped the shotrope and began hauling himself up through the broken deck levels, and within a minute he was standing on the upper deck, a hand on the shotrope, on the edge of the hole he'd blown a couple of days ago. Just a moment he paused, gazing around for the last time – a momentous moment – believing he would never see this grim scene ever again. It was in that instant, as he was about to telephone the surface to hoist away, that a rending crescendo of sound boomed against his eardrums through his mask and hood.

A sudden press of water made him look up where the coral-covered mainmast loomed within yards of him. In those seconds of peril he couldn't understand what was happening; but it seemed to him the entire wreck must be sliding under him, turning over, and that he was falling backwards into the bottom of the lagoon, falling ... falling ... until he was staring upwards from the perpendicular. Then a knife-edge realisation stabbed his mind into activity. It was not he that was falling – *it was the mast!*

Thirty feet or more of fossilised timber, broad as a barrel, was heeling over on to him. Under water, in a strange element and environment, a man's natural instincts were stifled, his thinking slowed up, and vital moments passed as the juggernaut beam swept down on him. Here was the cause of those quakes within the wreck. The mast must have been on the verge of collapse for days. It would have to fall one day and, weakened no doubt by the dynamite blasts, weighted by coral, the tug of the snatch block and strop, and even by the unusual currents, it was toppling at last – on him!

The great pillar descended in slow motion, blowing Dirk before

it on a pressure wave, coming so close to his divemask he could see minute coral structures and various mollusc shells, anemones and weeds on it. The pressure wave might have saved him, but as the mast fell across his lines they snatched him back under it. He felt a giant tug; then his shoulders were striking coral, his suit was ripping, water was drenching his neck, and there was a ringing din in his ears as his tank was jammed.

He must have been insensible for a time, perhaps only for seconds; then he was opening his eyes and seeing dimly through a disturbed fog of debris – fragments of coral, weeds, shells and tiny fish and sea animals darting about agitatedly – and he could hear himself gasping for air!

He was lying on his right side, almost on his face, crushed into the coral, and he was suffocating. No air was coming from his demand valve!

Some primeval instinct of self-preservation sent his fingers groping for the high-pressure valve control at the base of his emergency tank. His frozen fingers felt enormous and unwieldy; there was a pain growing as large as a grouper in his chest, and his mind was beginning to spin in fiery circles; then he turned the screw and his aching lungs drew air from the demand valve. He lay for fully a minute, just breathing.

At length his mind began working again and he strove to be calm about his predicament. He was held down by the mast, but not in great pain whatever injuries he might have. His agony had been from suffocation and temporarily that was cured. There was water under his chin, entering through a rip in his suit, and rising slightly from the way he was lying.

'On deck!' he gasped. 'On deck!'

There was no reply.

His telephone was dead; that meant his lifeline had been cut on the coral by the mast, and his airhose must have been severed too, because he was getting no surface supply and was breathing on his emergency tank. He wondered if he were hurt badly; he might have broken limbs and not know it for shock and cold.

The pearler skipper tried moving his limbs. One leg was free but his right leg was doubled under him and held fast. He wondered if his diving boot was bearing the weight of the mast. One arm was free too, but his right one was held under him. And he had the impression his tank was bearing weight. He began to struggle and heave, wasting precious air in the process, but he managed to get his right arm from under his body. Now he knew his tank was jammed. He thought now that he was being held by his tank and his right boot. It was a wonder the tank hadn't ruptured. If it had exploded he would have been dead already.

Out of the corner of his divemask he could see lengths of rope sinking and coiling over him. It was the shotrope – it must have parted near the schooner or on it. Dirk struggled again to release his boot, but he was only wasting air in his efforts. His boot was gripped fast . . . his tank too!

He lay quiet, waiting. Jim would come down – but thirty-five cubic feet of air wouldn't last long at this depth. He had only minutes left – about five. . . .

Chapter Fifteen

A Hard Ascent

Jim was nearly twenty fathoms deep when he caught up with the bullion chest on the runner's spring-hook. His swimfins rested on the chest and he descended with it. On deck Gomez was letting the winch run at full throttle; he knew when to ease up because he had a warning piece of white tape on the runner at twenty-six fathoms.

Gripping the cold runner Jim peered into the gloom below, and eventually his straining eyes discerned the bleak contours of the wreck. He had no clear impression of a ship at all, nor ever had, his attention was concentrated solely on a spot where air bubbles were rising in weak bursts out of coils of rope which were festooned over a huge grey beam. He knew it must be a mast or a spar but it looked like a fallen stone column.

The bullion chest, checked already by Gomez, decended on the coral deck with an iron thud. Jim automatically gave a heavy shake on the runner as a signal he had touched bottom. His heart was pounding dully, whether with the great air pressure he was breathing or with tension or both, he couldn't know.

A-shiver with the brutal cold, he kept his eyes on the escaping air, thrust himself away from the runner and swam the few feet to the mast. Dragging himself over it he found Dirk jammed under the mast, half-hidden by coils of rope.

Jim wasted a minute or two clearing the shotrope; then he got down on his knees so that Dirk could see him; and the pearler skipper gripped his belt and made a signal for him to come close to talk. By putting their heads together they could talk – at least Dirk could, because he was wearing a full facemask with his mouth free. Jim had a mouthpiece and a separate mask, but he could hear because water is a good conductor of sound.

'Airhose gone – breathing from – tank – only minutes,' Dirk muttered. 'I'm fast – my tank – and my right boot!'

Jim turned first to his skipper's trapped boot, groping about with numbed hands under the mast. He found the boot and tried to haul on it. Then he felt Dirk's grip on his harness and he leaned his head close to his skipper's again. Dirk was breathing hoarsely. He wasn't getting sufficient air because his tank regulator had been injured. He struggled to speak.

'*Unbuckle the boot!*'

Again Jim groped and this time he found the buckle and released it. Then he tugged on Dirk's rubber-suited leg, and the skipper tugged as well, and his foot came out of the jammed boot, leaving it for ever under the mast.

Now Jim turned to the tank which was held fast; then he stopped, staring helplessly for a moment, horrifyingly conscious of the flying seconds and the nerve-wrecking depth, and the mindless hostility of the pressing fathoms. There was no time to release that tank. Even if it was released it wouldn't be any good, because there would be no air left in it. Minutes had passed and now, just two or three remained. There was only one source of air, his own.

On his knees, beside his skipper, Jim removed his mouthpiece and held it in front of the other's divemask. He pointed to the surface, then he replaced his mouthpiece to take a few relieving breaths, and leaning close he pointed urgently to the surface again.

'I understand,' the pearler skipper said weakly. Straightaway he began to pull at the release clasp that would unbuckle his tank harness in one motion. He dragged a last hard breath from the failing tank. Then his unfeeling fingers tugged at the bands holding his mask and hood in place. He pulled them off. The icy sea drenched his face. He couldn't see properly any more, just a confused haze, and his terrible plight was relieved by just one thing –

Jim giving him the mouthpiece of his own twin-tank equipment.

Dirk breathed on the waterlung – once – twice – three times. And it was the hardest thing in his life to remove the mouthpiece, for without his mask he was like a half-drowned man and his vision was just a confusing chaos of grey objects shuddering like trees in a gale.

But Jim was helping him upright as Dirk instinctively conserved his breath. They went half swimming, half walking and Jim seized the runner. Again he passed the mouthpiece. Stoically both divers restrained their clamouring instincts to obey a routine they had often practised, had indeed once used before in an emergency, but at only a quarter of this depth. Each took three breaths on the shared mouthpiece, exhaling the last one very slowly.

When Jim gripped the runner he managed to give it a series of tugs, meant to be a 'double-four' signal to haul up. Whatever it was Gomez and O'Hara interpreted it aright, probably because they could imagine no other meaning. The box of gold began to rise, carrying the two semi-drowned divers with it.

By the time they had got half-way on the ascent they were both drilled in the spartan exercise of exchanging the mouthpiece of Jim's double 'seventy' outfit. Jim was exhausted and Dirk was in a worse state, battered physically and mentally by his ordeal, and his unprotected eyes began to smart with the cold and salt water, until the pain grew unbearable and he had to keep them shut, blinking them open only when the mouthpiece was exchanged.

Then, in the lightening sea, Jim sighted the *Jolo*'s hull. For Dirk it could be dangerous, even fatal, if he were hoisted clear to the surface without any decompression, for he had been down so long he might collapse with the bends. But there was nothing Jim could do to stop this happening, because Gomez and O'Hara obviously did not know who or what they were lifting. So in another minute both divers broke surface in a swell running deep along the schooner's hull.

Dirk had the mouthpiece at this moment and as soon as Jim could draw a breath he shouted, 'Stop hoisting!'

O'Hara was half-way down the diving ladder, watching like a hawk and his booming voice echoed the mate's command to Gomez. And they were held there, precariously awash on the bullion chest, while Jim lashed his weary, frozen, pallid-faced skipper to the runner with the remaining fragment of his lifeline. Then he unlatched his harness and struggled free of his tanks, and he saw Dirk had the mouthpiece and the divemask pulled over his eyes, and the tanks clutched to his chest.

'Lower away – three fathoms!' he cried, and as the runner slipped away down again Jim let go of it and made for the diving ladder. O'Hara, strong as a bear, hauled the mate out of the sea and helped him aboard. Meanwhile Gomez had stopped the winch and hitched the runner on the drum.

'Keep him down there,' Jim managed to gasp to the others. 'He's safe.' But as soon as he was recovered enough to take charge he ordered the severed airhose to be hauled in and a spare mouthpiece to be fitted. Dirk must have at least half an hour's decompression, and he would soon need a new air supply because the tanks they had both been using would not last much longer.

A few minutes later they hauled Dirk up to ten feet under the boat, where they could see him, and Jim went down again with another divemask and the surface airhose. In the pale amethyst water he found his skipper, sitting astride the bullion chest, minus one boot, breathing modestly from the mouthpiece of the double tanks which he was holding against his chest. Once more they exchanged their breathing equipment and Jim surfaced with the almost empty tanks, leaving Dirk with the surface airhose.

The day was nearly done when Dirk was eventually brought up together with the last of the *San Nicolas*'s bullion, and there was never such a feeling of relief for a skipper to come aboard his ship.

'Death was near that time, Señor Rogers,' Gomez said quietly when they helped the pearler skipper to the diving bench, and the Filipino spoke for them all.

Dirk was cut and bruised and badly shaken up and after a hot drink to restore his circulation he was thankful to get into his bunk. That night passed peacefully and when morning came the skipper

was feeling a great deal better, and both he and Jim were beginning to see their experiences in retrospect. It wouldn't be too long before those nightmare minutes on the *San Nicolas* were just another diving yarn in some out-of-the-way harbour on their travels.

The weather stayed unkindly, but they spent the day quite un-eventfully clearing up their gear and attending to their diving equipment. Towards evening they picked up their moorings and set sail. Dirk took the schooner under auxiliary motor power through the grumbling tides of the reef passage, and he waited until they were well clear of broken water by two cable lengths before he put the helm a-weather and brought his craft on a north-easterly head-ing.

'See yonder!' O'Hara called out suddenly, pointing a long arm astern as he stood by Dirk at the helm. 'Tell me, what's that on the lagoon?'

Dirk turned to look, and over the lurching taffrail he saw a phantom shape moving weirdly over the wind-snarled lagoon. As he watched the shadowy outline vanished, seeming to sink swiftly into the waters where the coral wreck lay submerged thirty fathoms deep.

'Another waterspout,' he said. 'That bluff must set up whirl-winds over the island.'

'Maybe and maybe not,' the Irishman growled with a super-stitious frown darkening his rugged face. 'I'm thinkin' it might be that old mad Spaniard takin' a farewell look at his gold – bound home, at last!'

'Cordovada will always haunt that island as long as there are folks like you to see him, O'Hara,' Dirk told the big fellow with a smile. 'Now then, let's get some sail hoisted before we roll the sticks out of her!'

In the long ocean-deep swells beyond the reefs the schooner was beginning to roll rail to rail, gunwales under, and at Dirk's direction they all put their backs into the job of running up jibs, fore- and mainsails. Under this hard press of canvas the craft settled down comfortably with the rising north-westerly wind on her quarter. The sun was by this time a great red cinder dipping below the western horizon, the sea waters were turning grimly grey, and the roll of surf on the island reefs was growing in volume as though drawing strength from the dying daylight.

Soon the harsh contours of Cordovada Island were moulded into a dark sunset-fettered shadow astern as the schooner, with her rigging taut and singing, her canvas booming, and spray lifting over her weather rail, carried Dirk and his crew back to Kunjang with their treasure trove.

More Beaver Books

We hope you have enjoyed this Beaver Book. Here are some of the other titles:

A Knight and his Castle   What it was like to live in a castle, by R. Ewart Oakeshott

Travel Quiz   A brain-teasing quiz book for all the family on all aspects of travel by plane, train and car

My Favourite Animal Stories   Sad, funny and exciting stories about all sorts of animals, chosen and introduced by Gerald Durrell

Who Knows?   Twelve unsolved mysteries involving sudden death, mysterious disappearances and hidden treasure, by Jacynth Hope-Simpson

The Call of the Wild   The epic story of Buck the great sledge dog in the frozen North, by Jack London

The Last of the Vikings   Henry Treece's exciting story, in the saga tradition, about the young Harald Hardrada, King of Norway; with superb illustrations by Charles Keeping

Ghost Horse   Dramatic story about a legendary stallion in the American West, by Joseph E. Chipperfield

New Beavers are published every month and if you would like the *Beaver Bulletin* – which gives all the details – please send a stamped addressed envelope to:

Beaver Bulletin
The Hamlyn Group
Astronaut House
Feltham
Middlesex TW14 9AR

319148